POKÉMON™

LEGENDARY POKÉMON

ViZ media

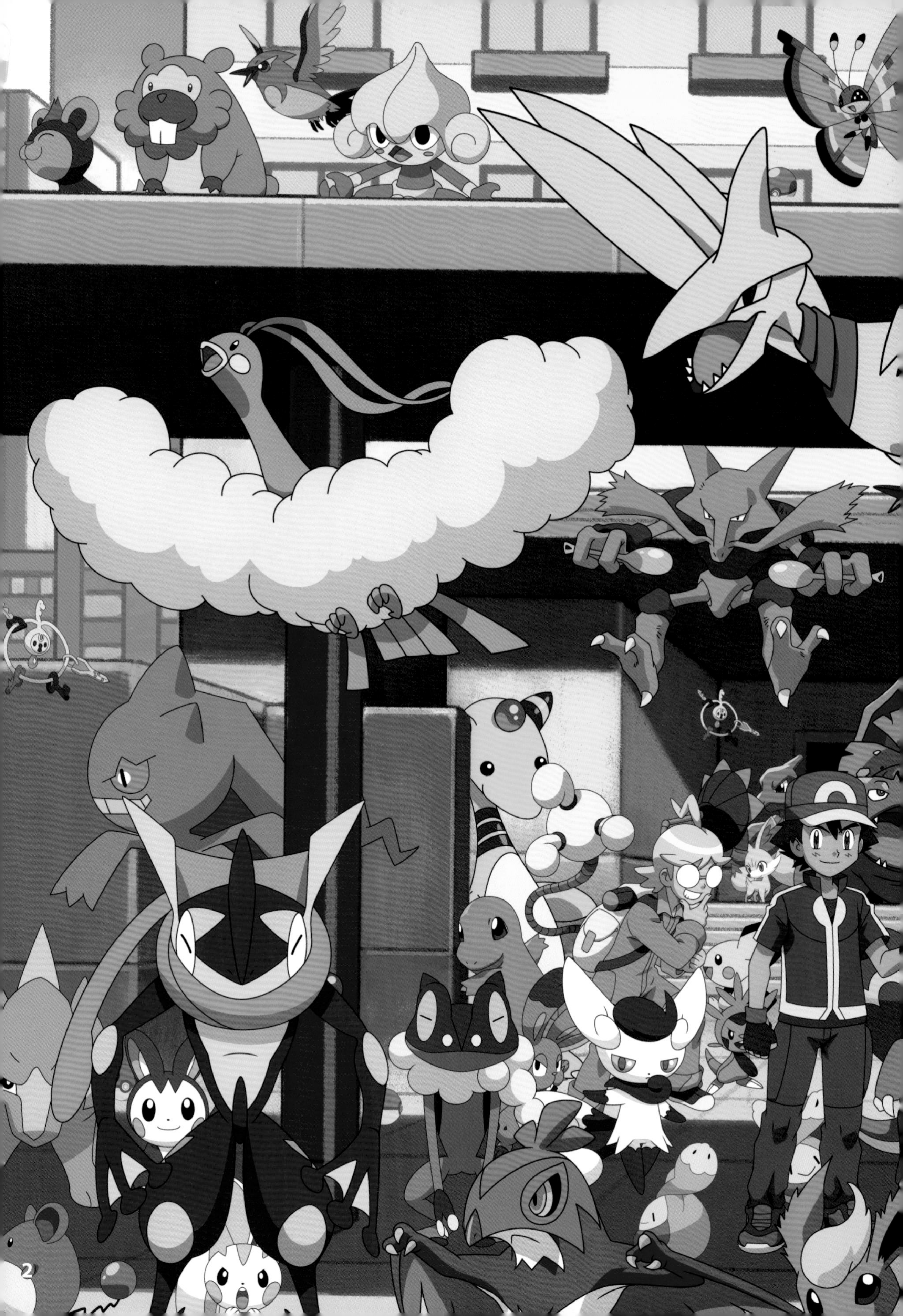

THE GREAT DEPARTURE

LOOK FOR... ×7

Ash, Serena, Clemont, and Bonnie set off for the forest, hoping to meet the Legendary Pokémon of the region. In the city, they run into a crowd of Pokémon ready to accompany them on this incredible adventure! But where is Pikachu in all this commotion?

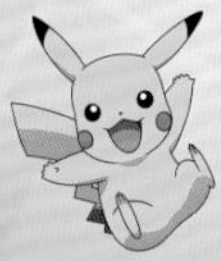

Pikachu

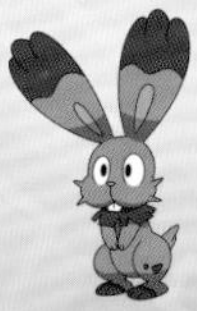

Bunnelby

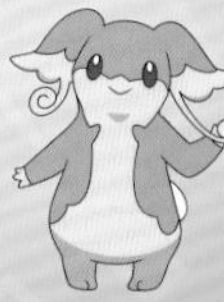

Audino

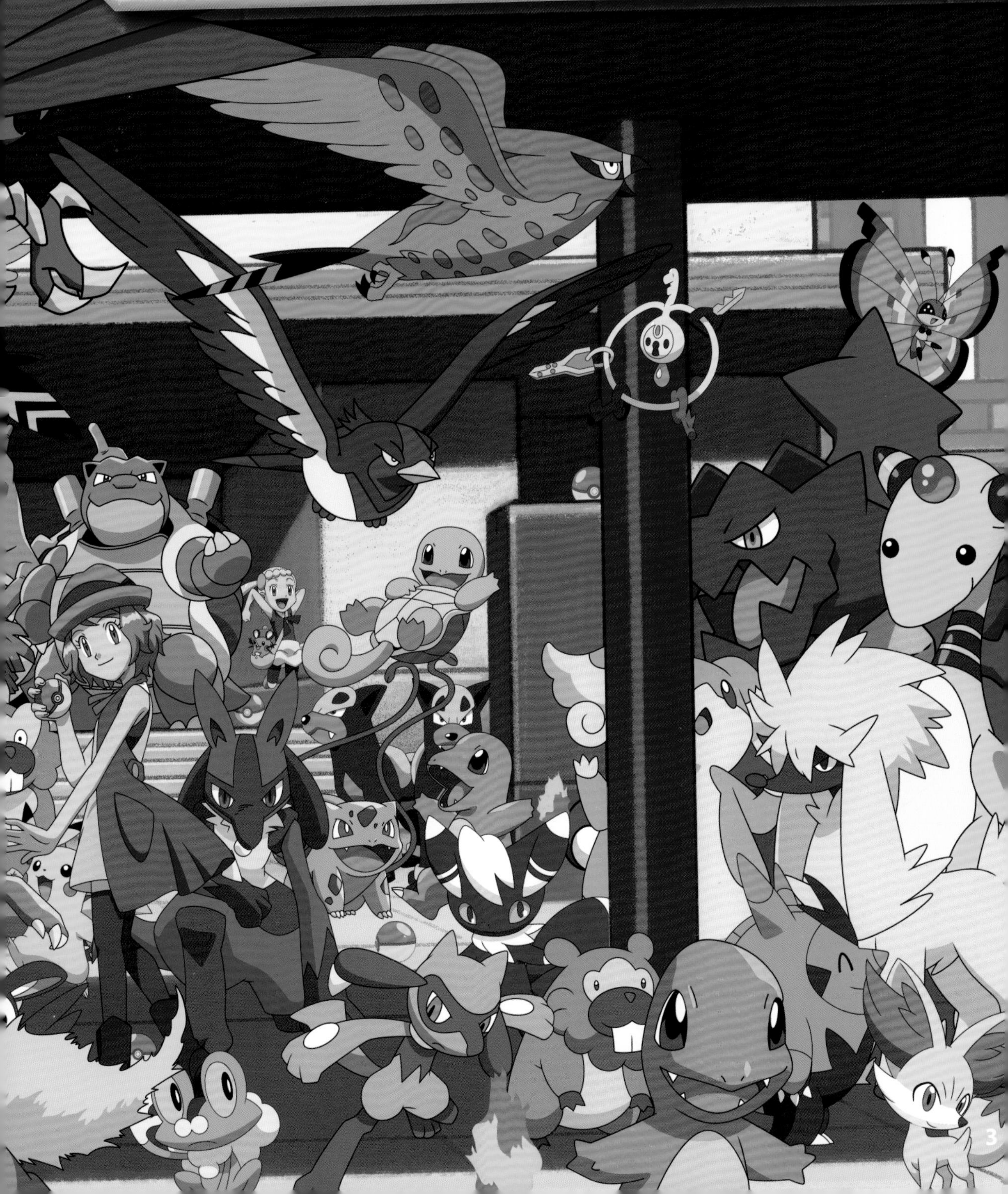

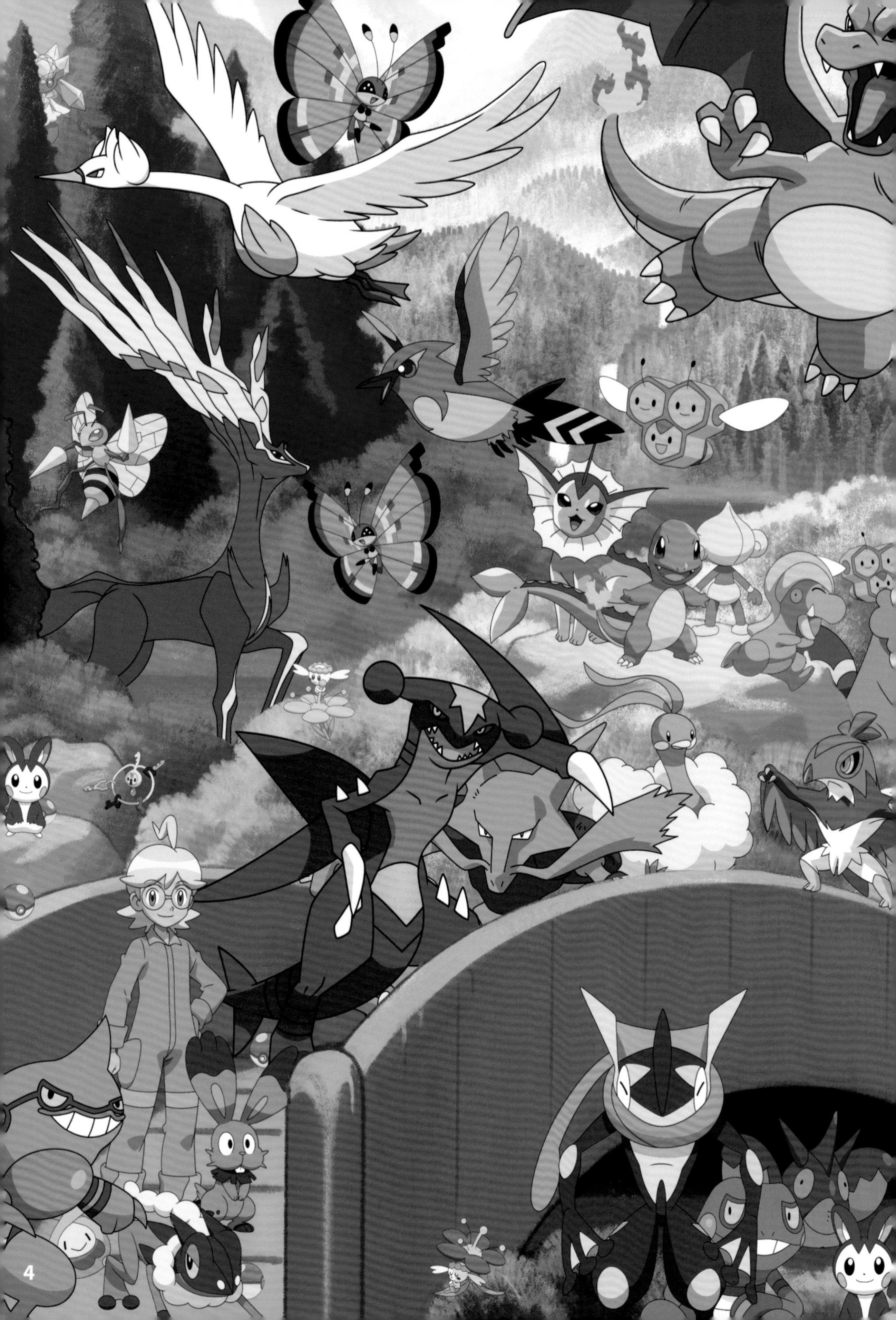

AT THE WATER'S EDGE

LOOK FOR... ×9

At the edge of the forest, Ash and his friends have an incredible encounter. They've spotted Xerneas, the Legendary Fairy-type Pokémon. But watch out! Don't lose track of the other Pokémon, who won't miss this opportunity to hide!

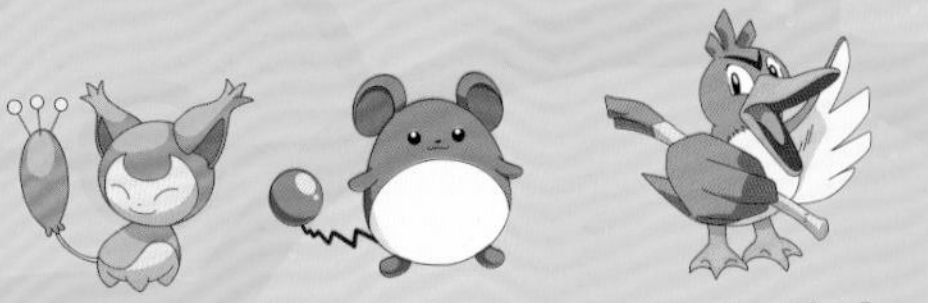

Skitty Marill Farfetch'd

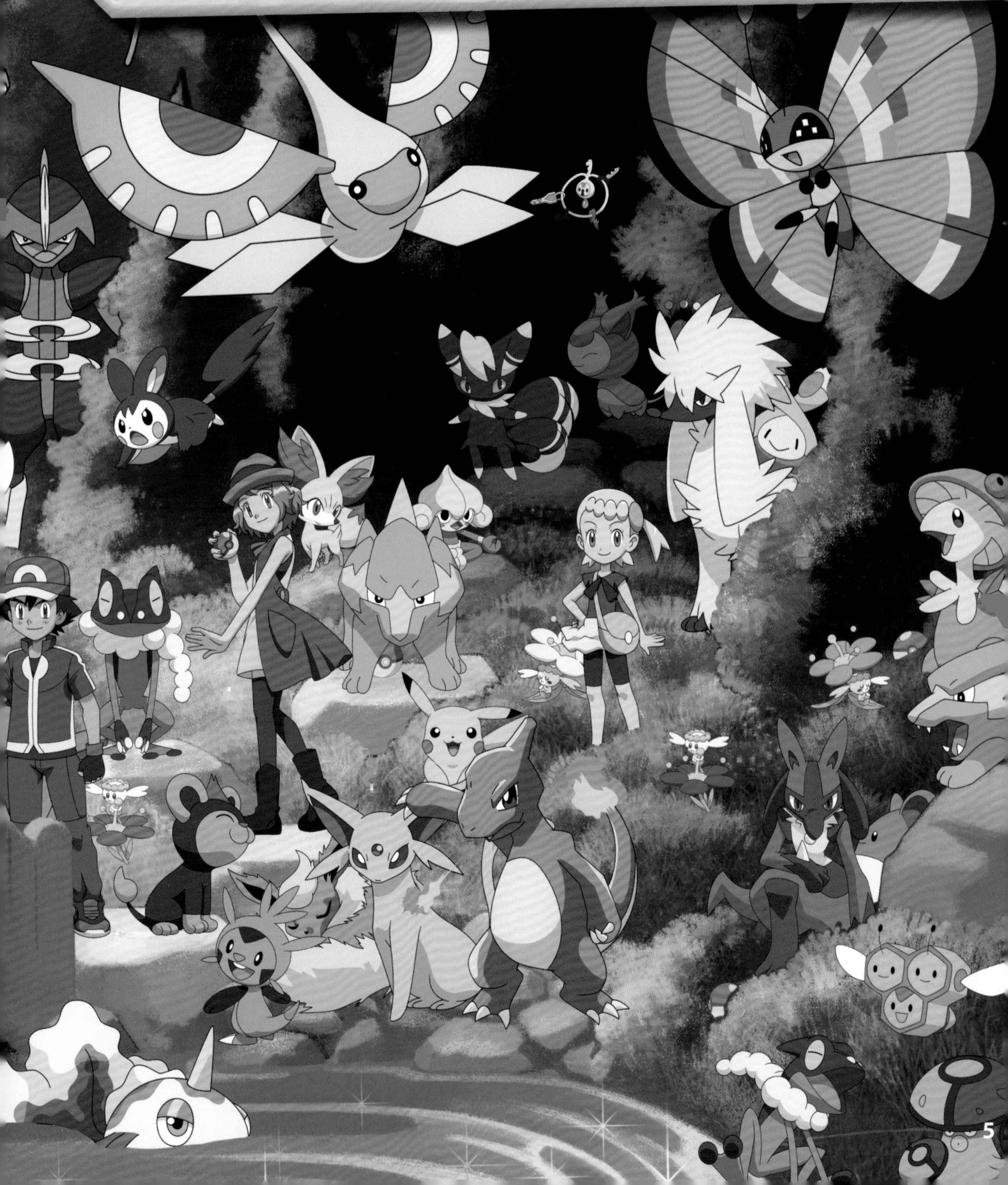

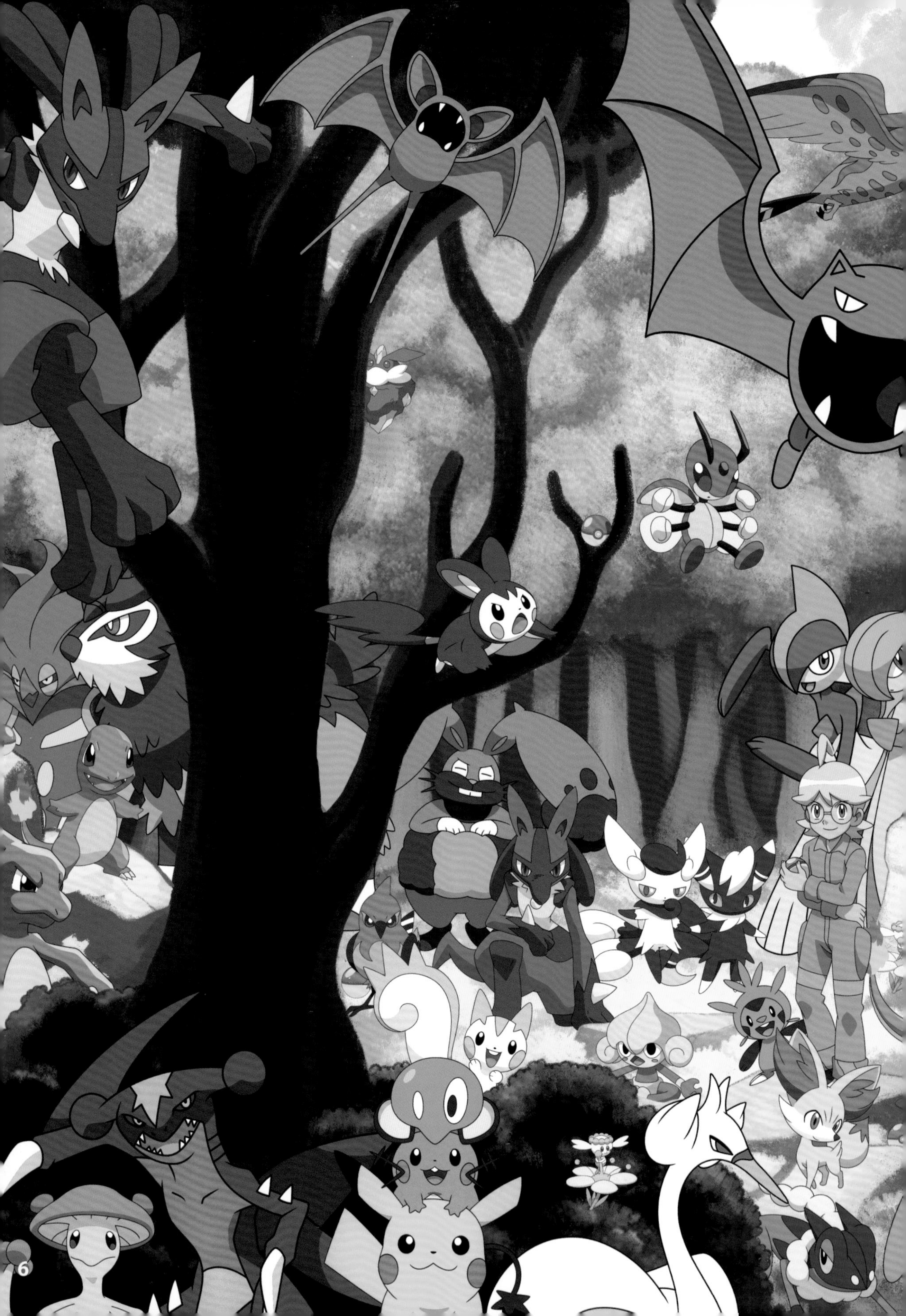

THE CLEARING

Farther along the path, Ash and his friends notice a new Pokémon! It looks like Zygarde Core! This new friend appears to be enjoying itself with Pikachu and Dedenne!

LOOK FOR...

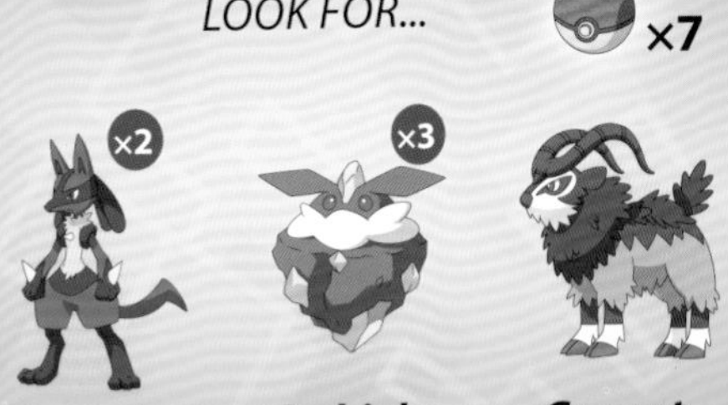
×7
×2
×3

Lucario Carbink Gogoat

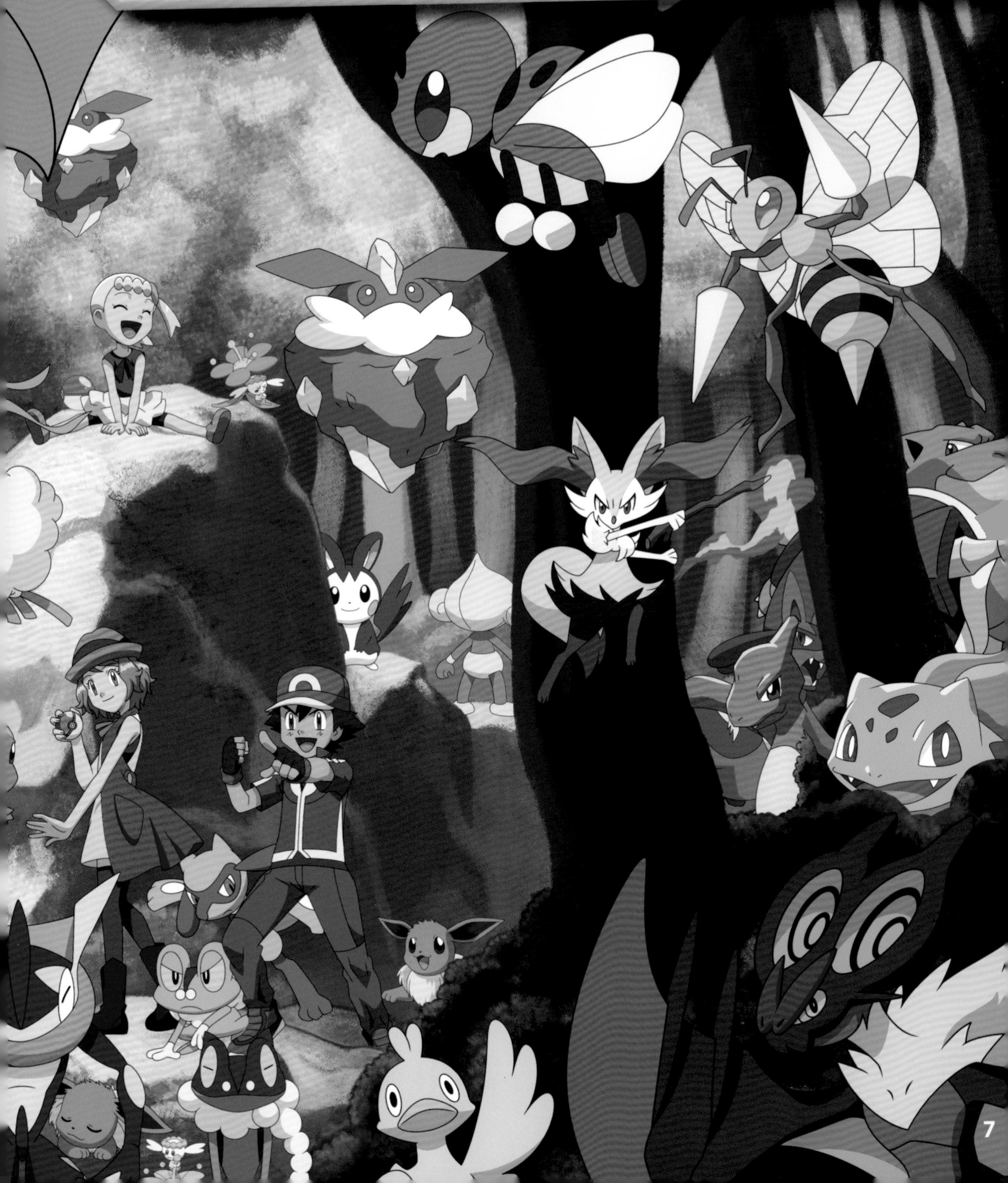

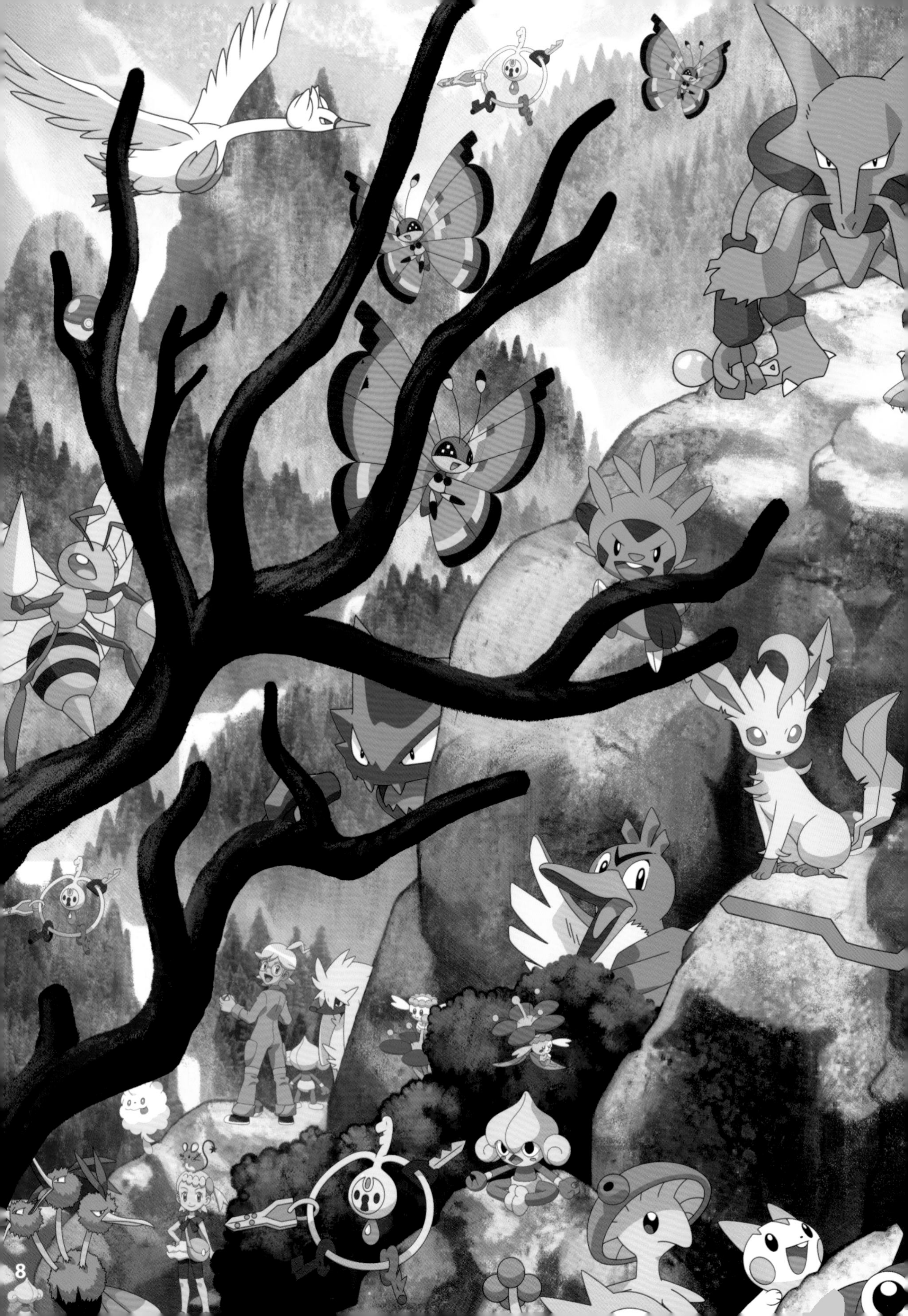

ON THE MOUNTAIN

Pikachu and Dedenne are sad to leave their new friend. However, on their way to the summit of the mountain, Ash and his friends come face-to-face with a Pokémon they've never seen before: Zygarde 10% Forme!

LOOK FOR...

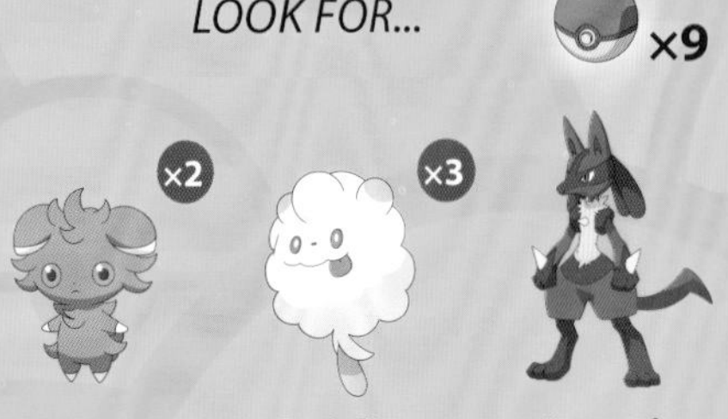

×9
×2
×3

Espurr **Swirlix** **Lucario**

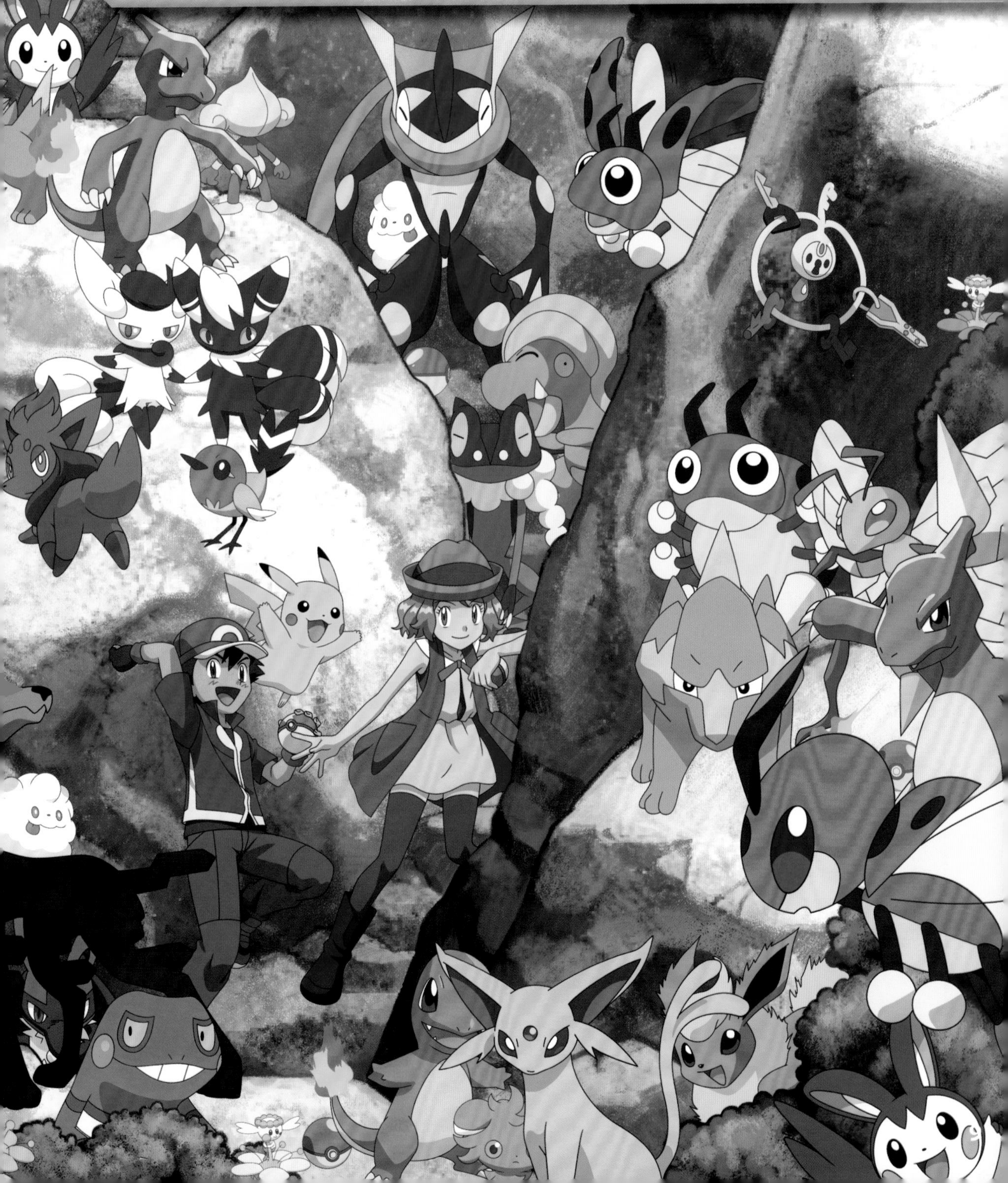

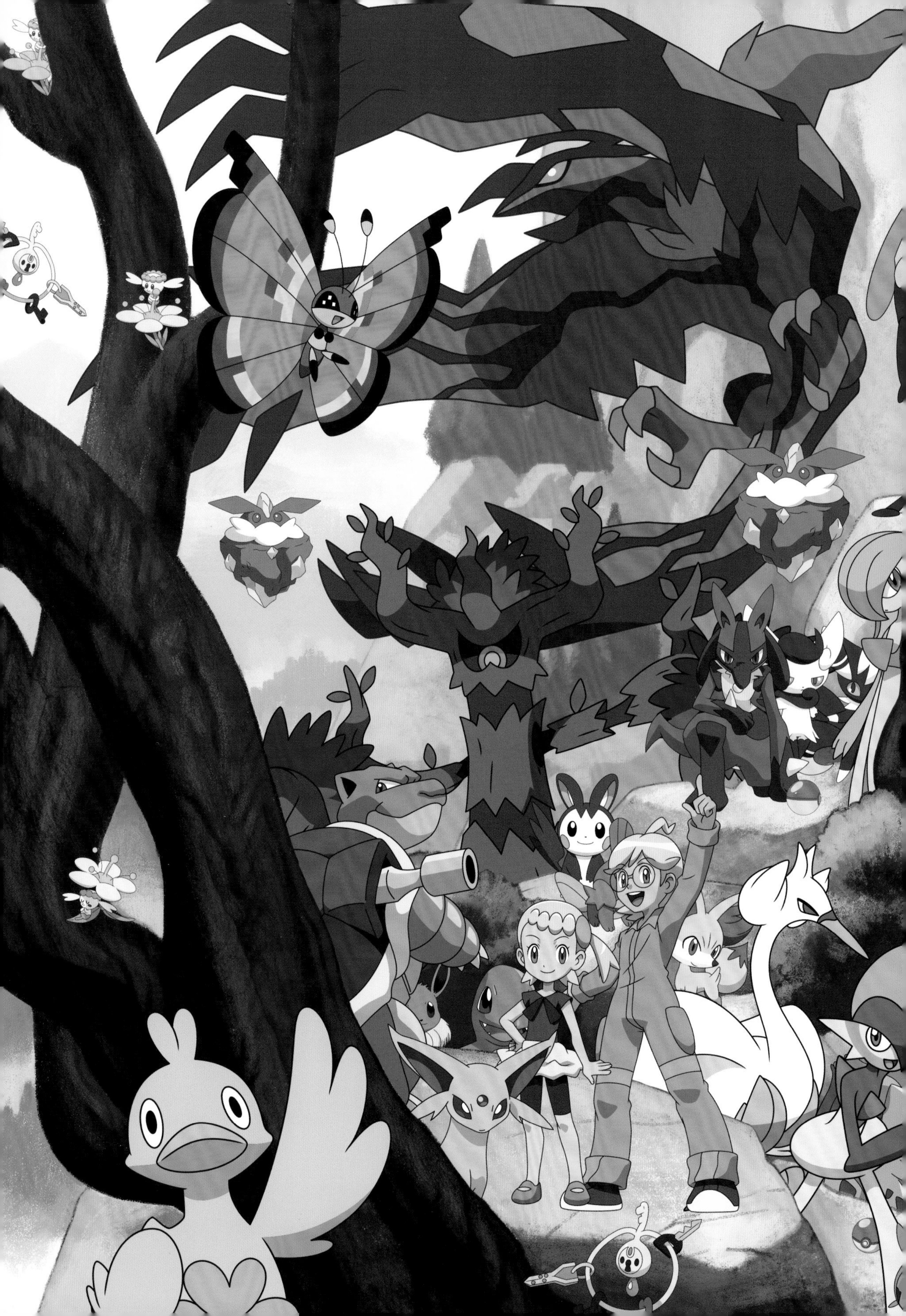

MEETING AT THE SUMMIT

LOOK FOR... 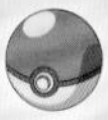 ×5

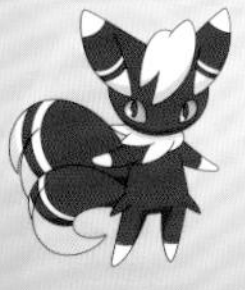
Meowstic♂

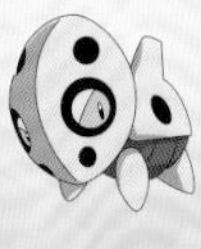
Aron

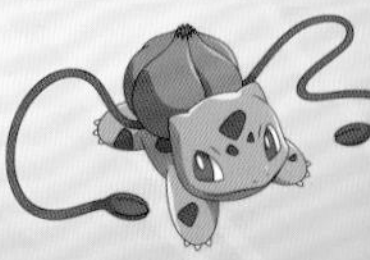
Bulbasaur

Our Trainer friends are about to enter a cave when, all of a sudden, the powerful Yveltal makes an appearance. This Legendary Pokémon takes everyone by surprise, even astonishing the crowd of Pokémon!

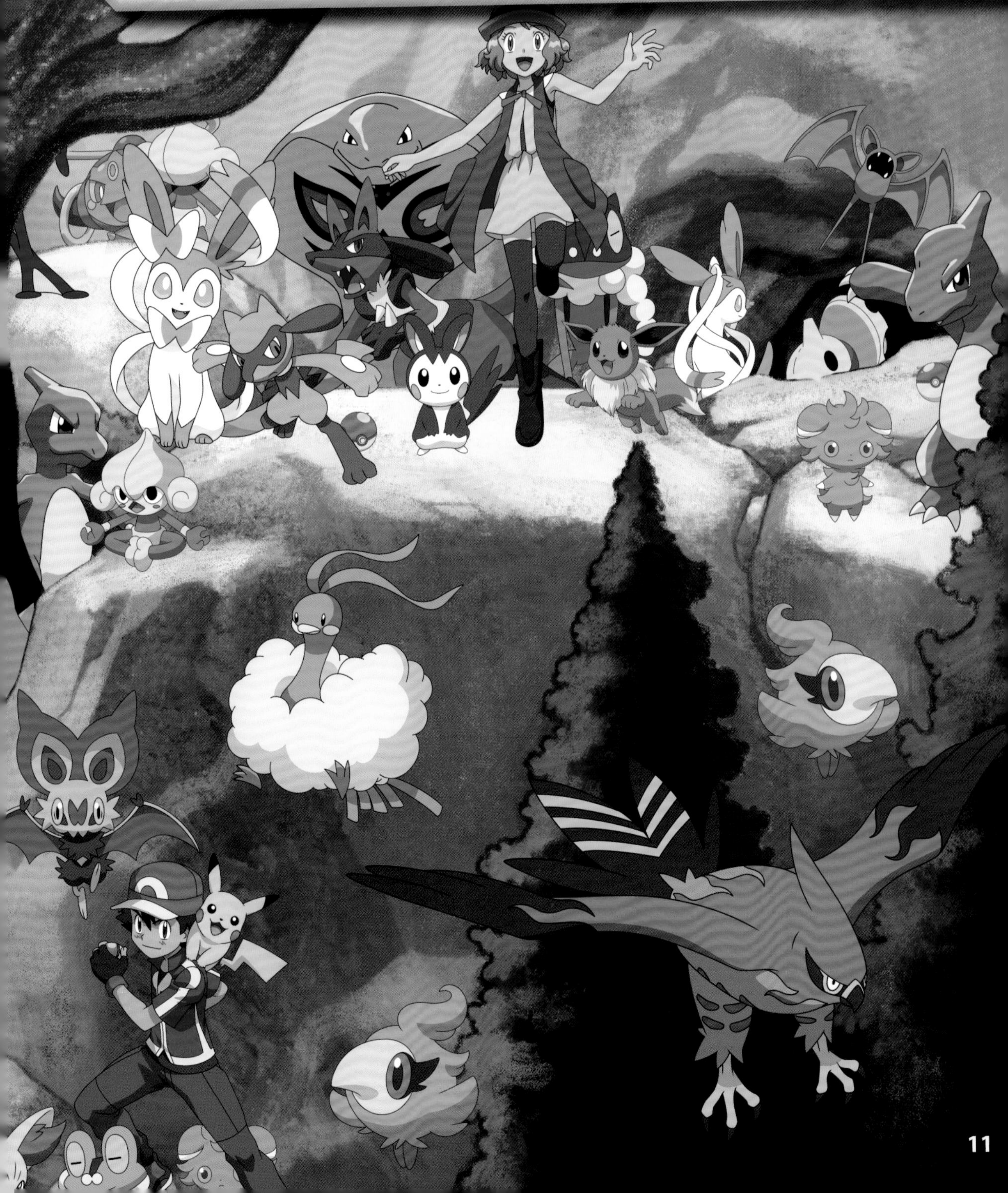

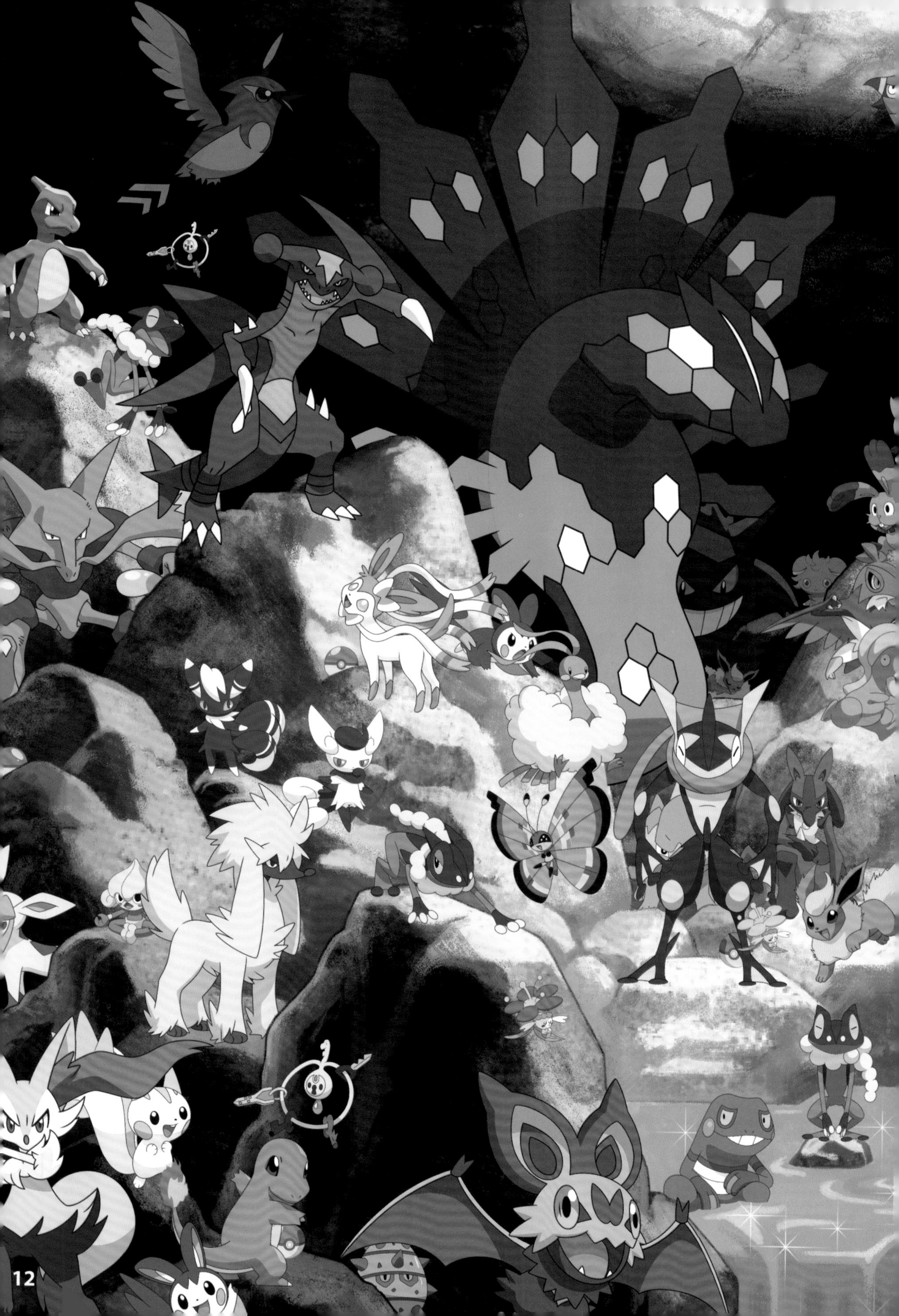

IN THE CAVE

Ash and his friends continue their trek, hoping for a chance to see Zygarde, Legendary Pokémon of Kalos. Once they've reached the back of the cave, they discover Zygarde's den. Our Trainer friends are so happy they forget about the Pokémon hiding in the shadows!

LOOK FOR...

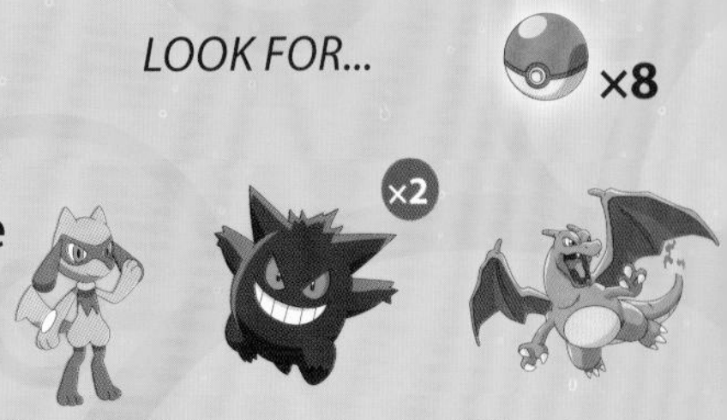

×8
×2

Riolu Gengar Charizard

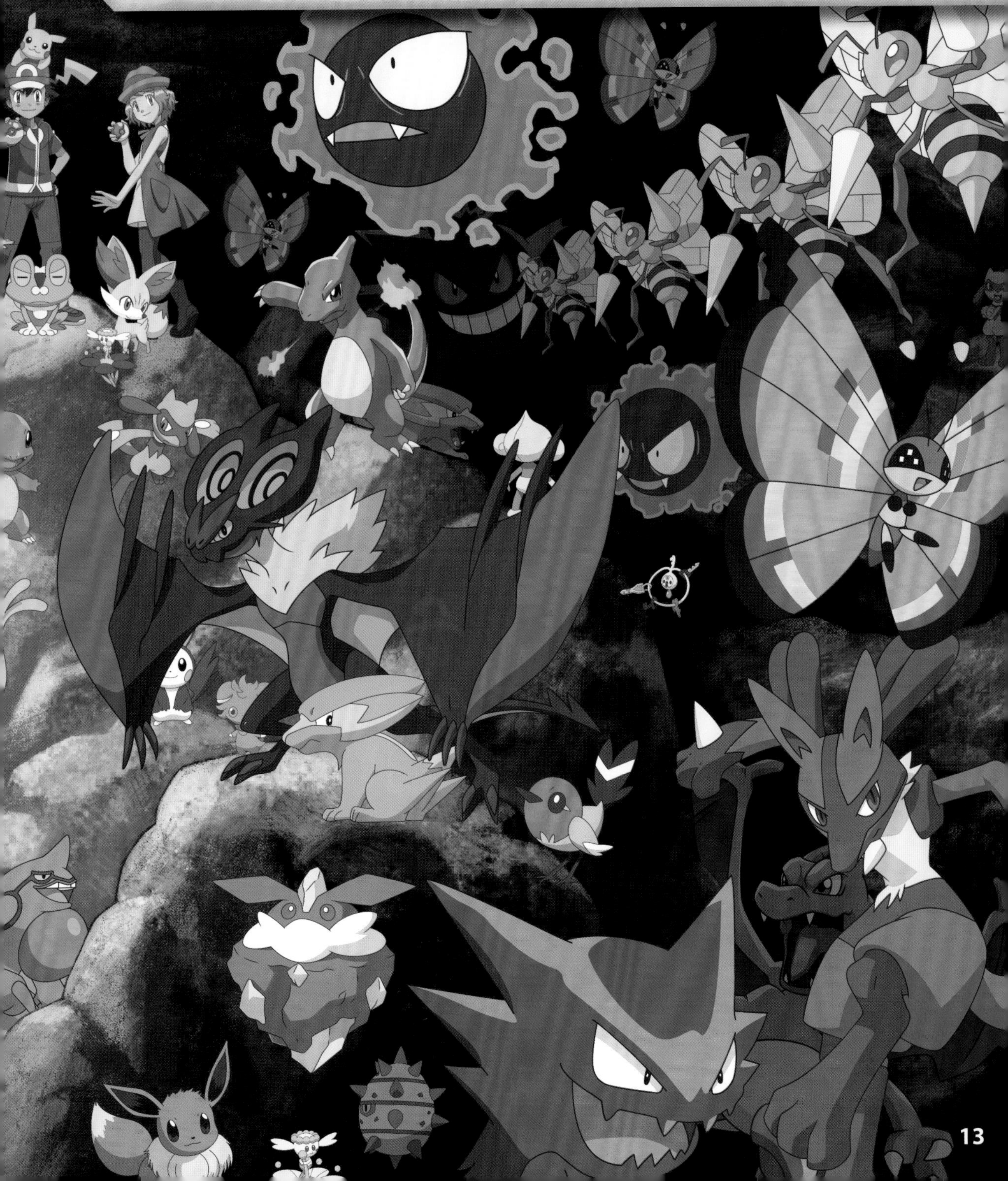

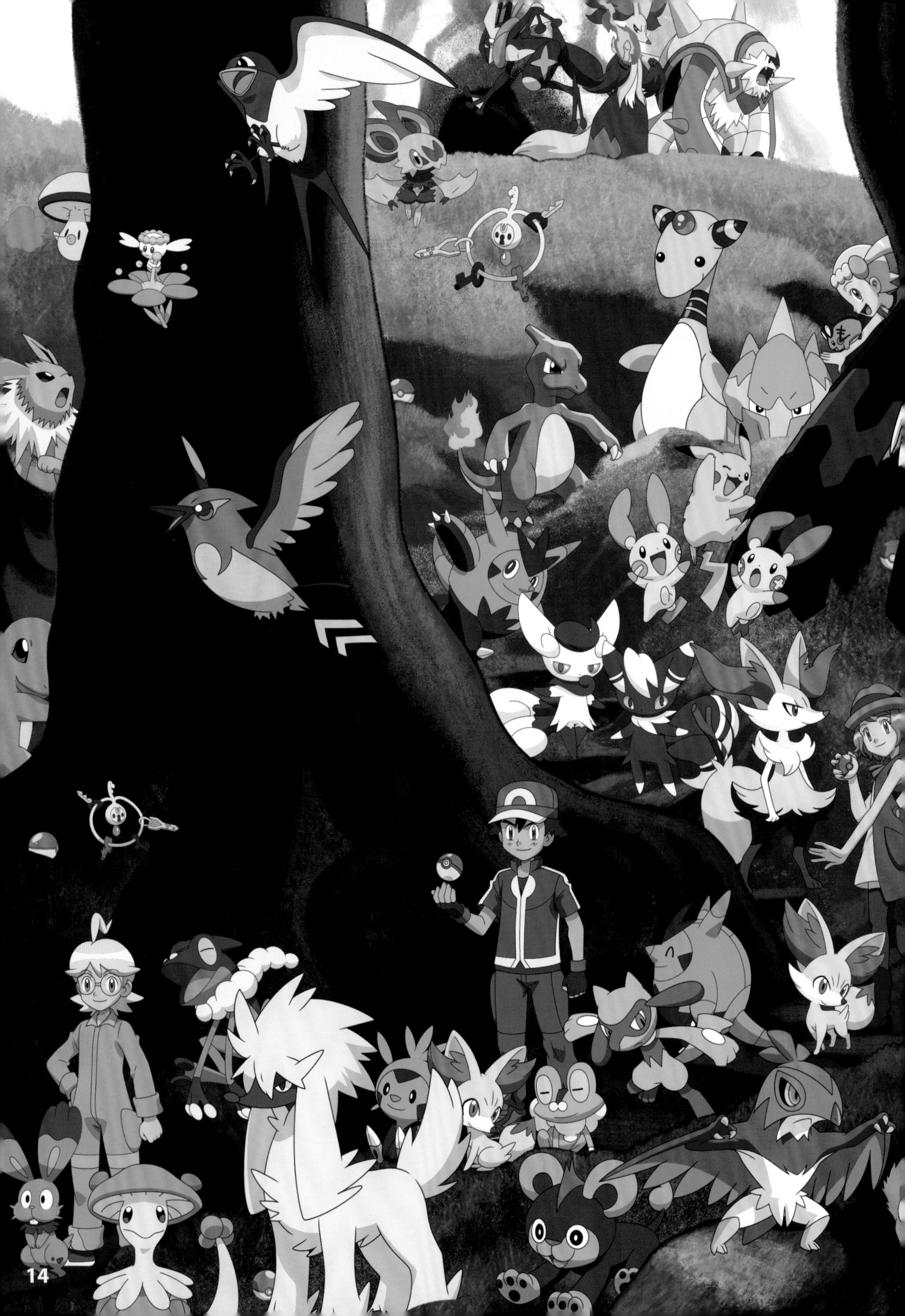

WOODSON

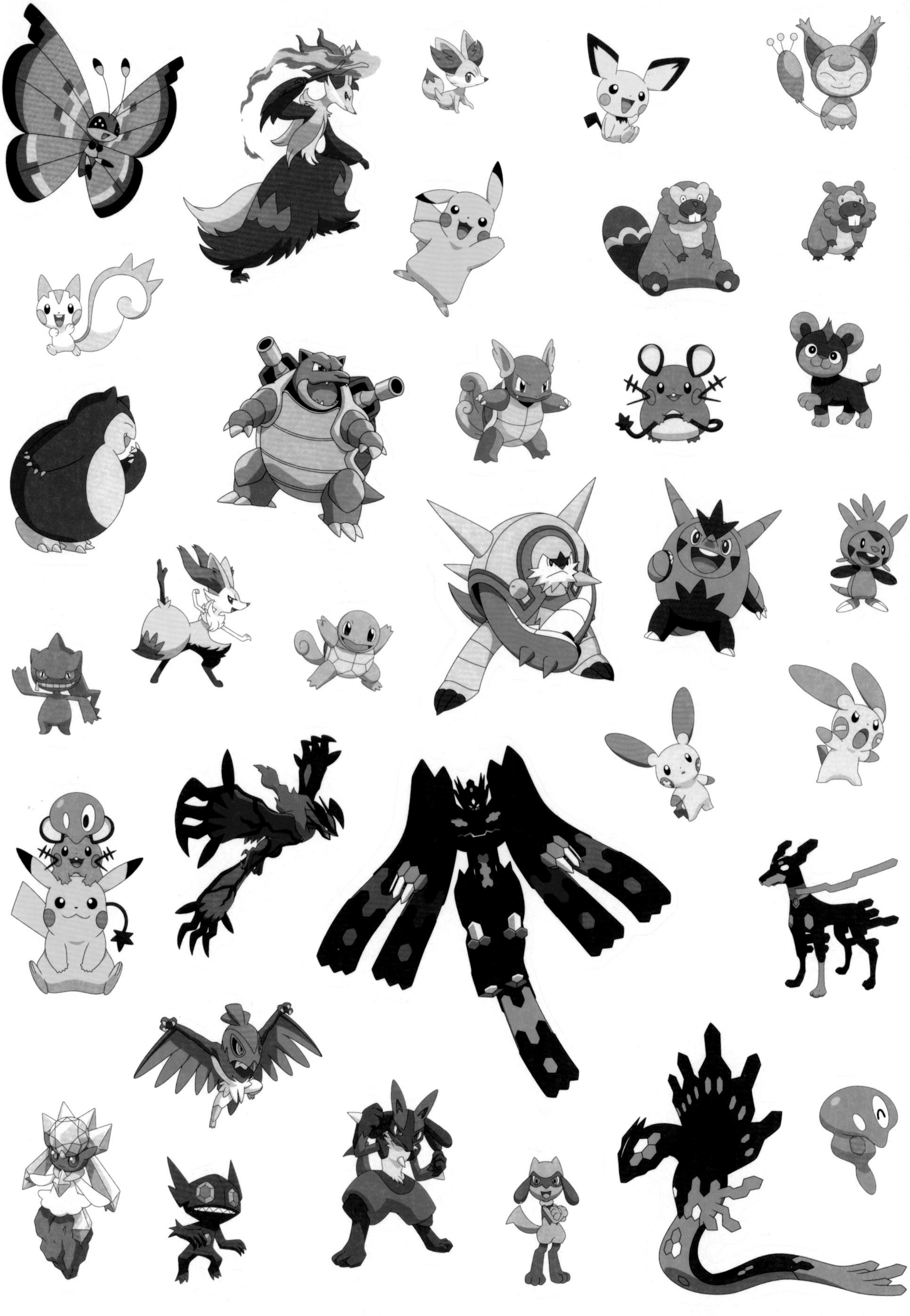

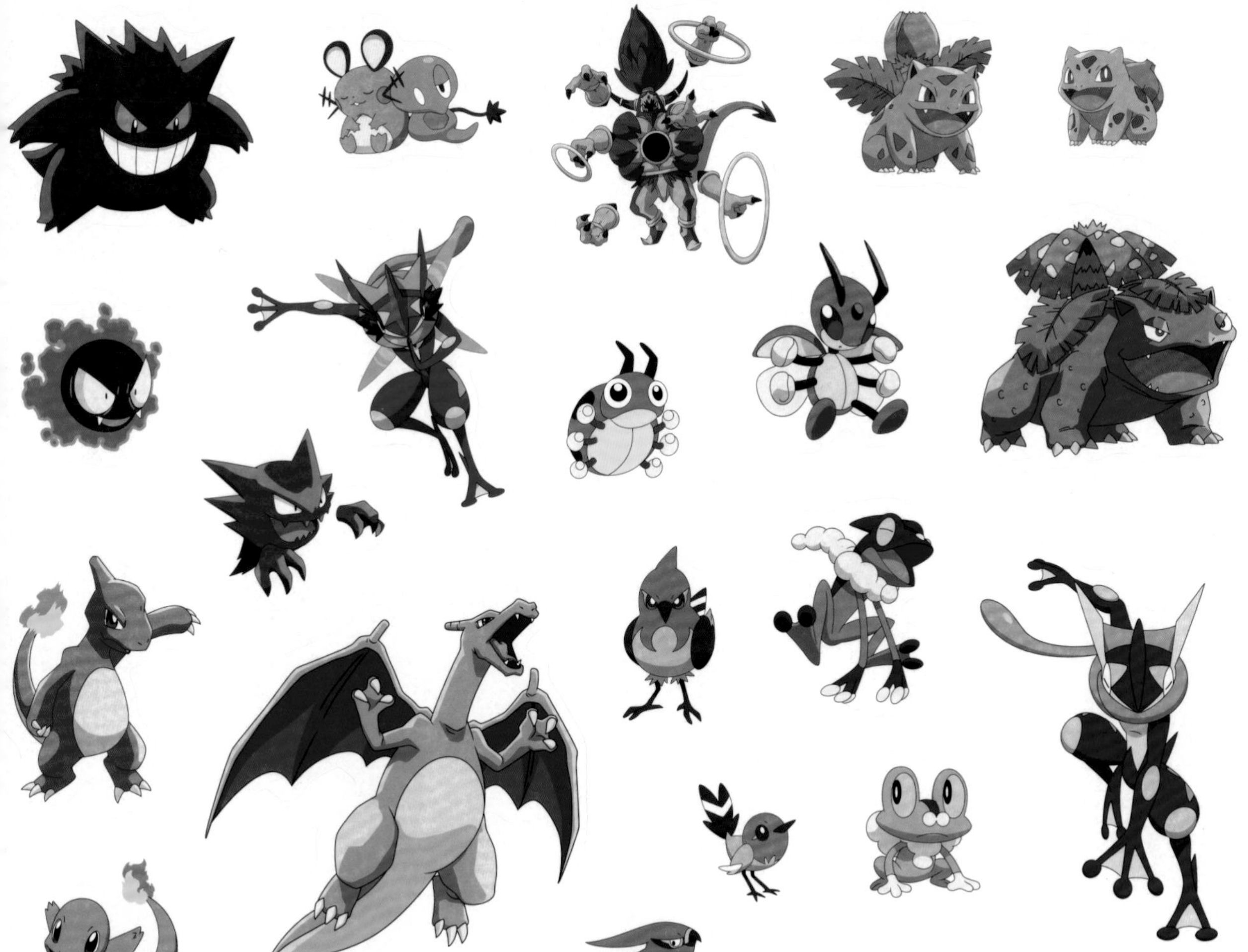

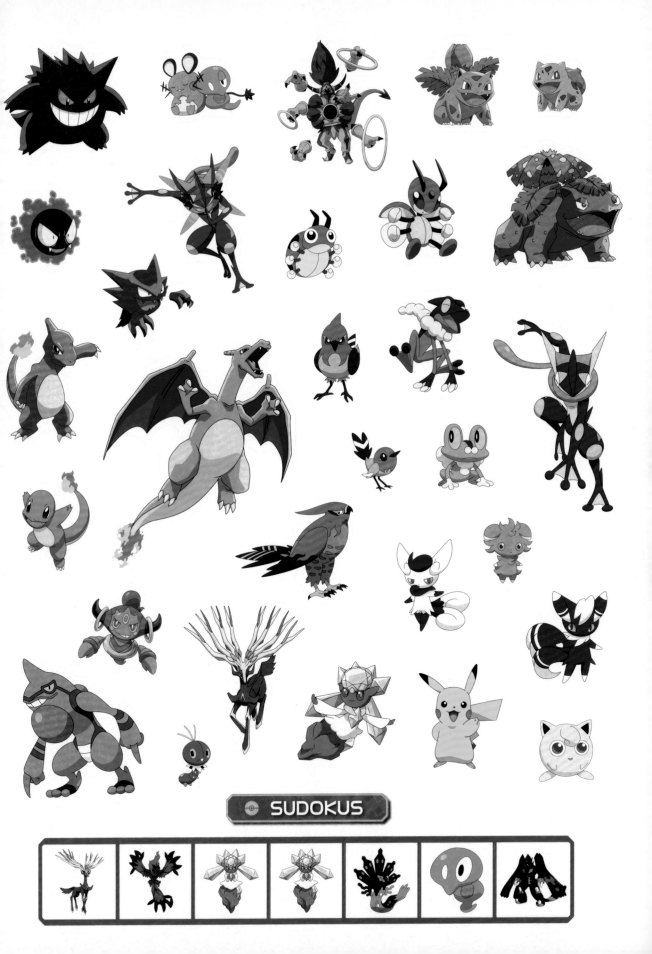

SUDOKUS

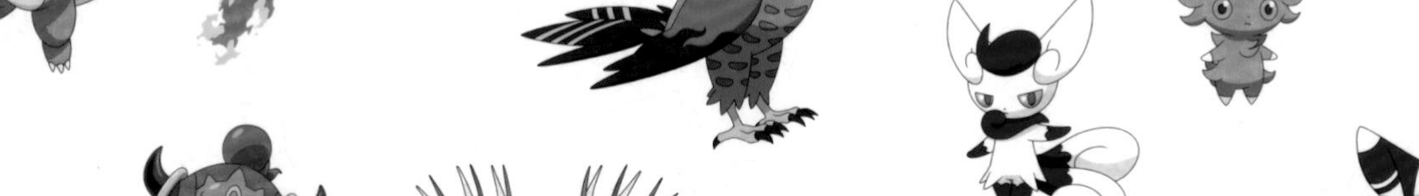

A FINAL SURPRISE

Our friends are on their way home, happy to have met so many new Pokémon, when they come face-to-face with yet another Forme of Zygarde—its Complete Forme! It's incredible. They've now seen so many Formes of this Pokémon! How lucky!

LOOK FOR...

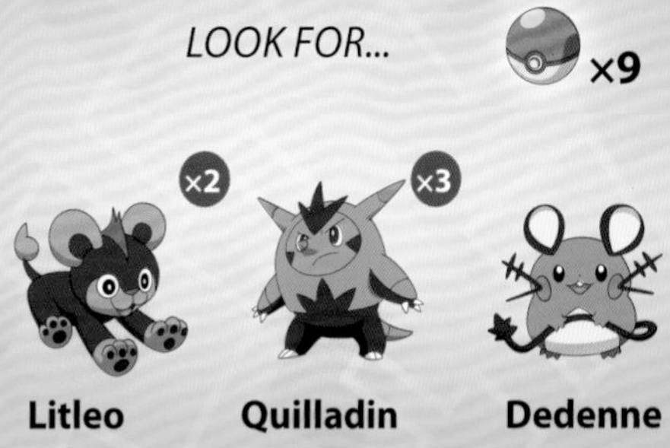
×9
×2
×3
Litleo
Quilladin
Dedenne

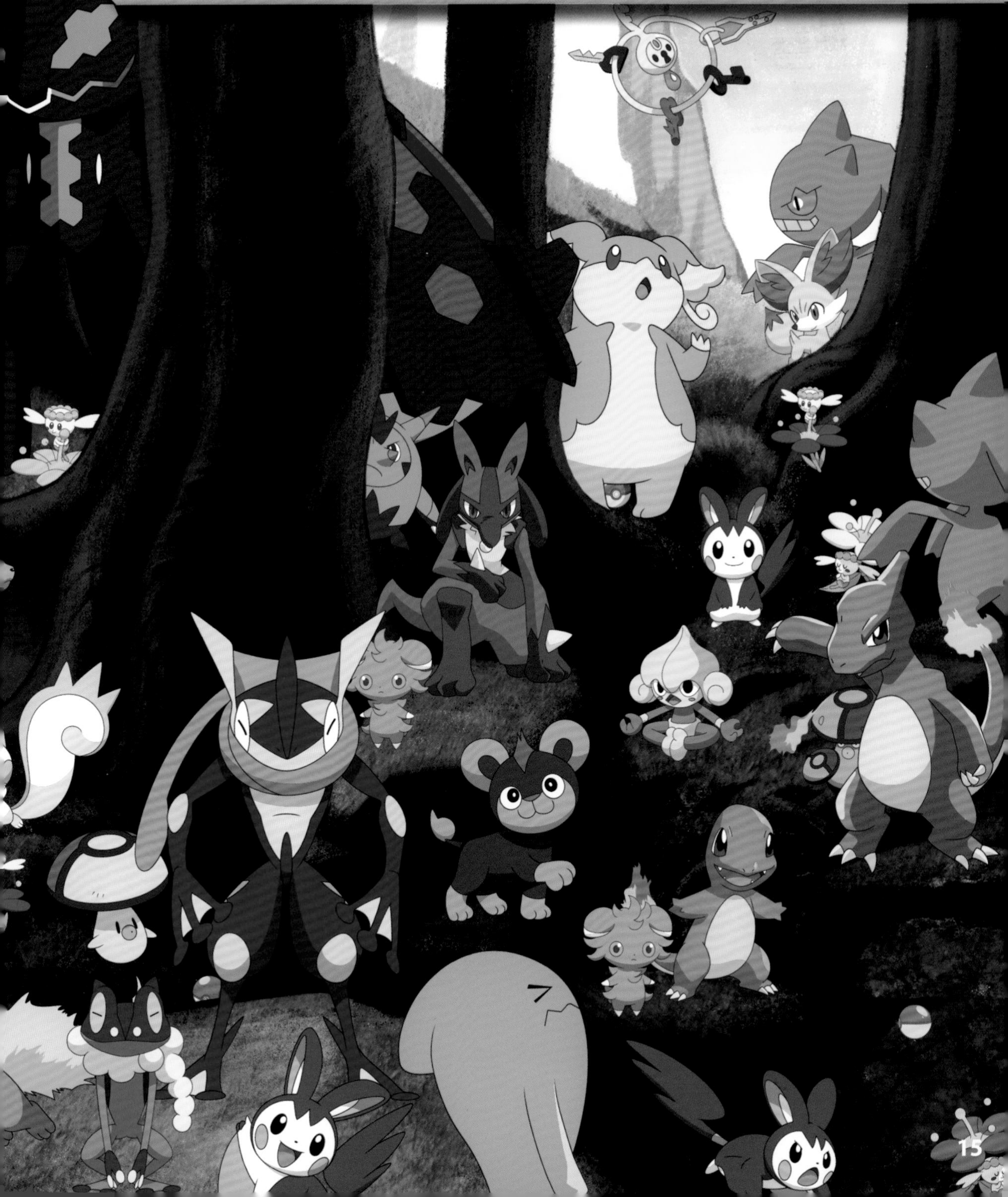

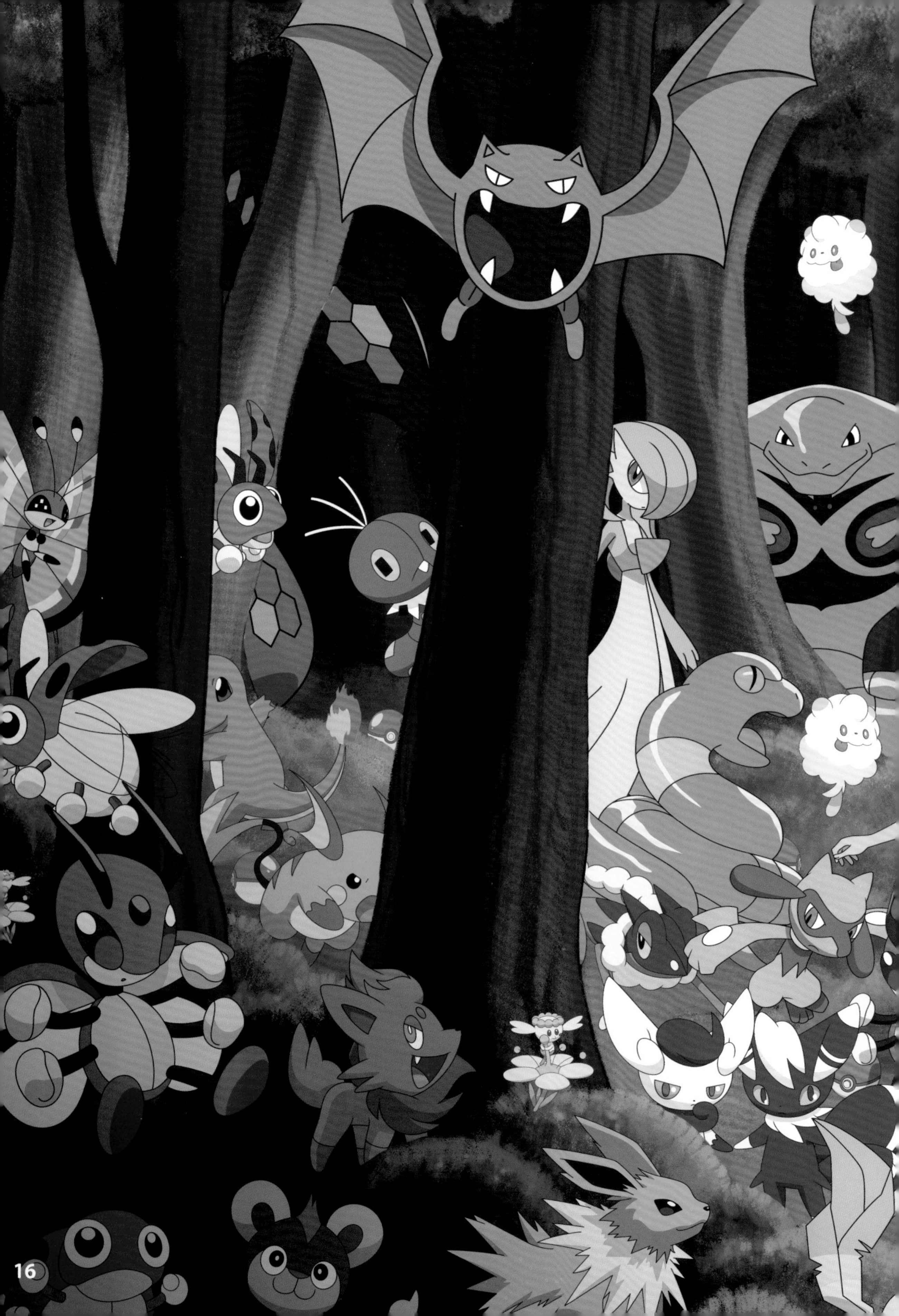

A MEMORABLE ADVENTURE

LOOK FOR... ×9

The sun sets. Our four heroes have realized their dreams and then some! All kinds of Pokémon have accompanied them on their return, but it looks like Xerneas, Yveltal, and Zygarde are hiding in the woods. Can you find them?

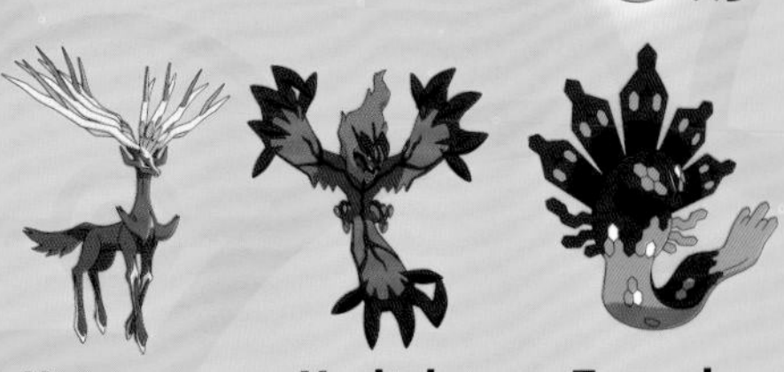

Xerneas **Yveltal** **Zygarde**

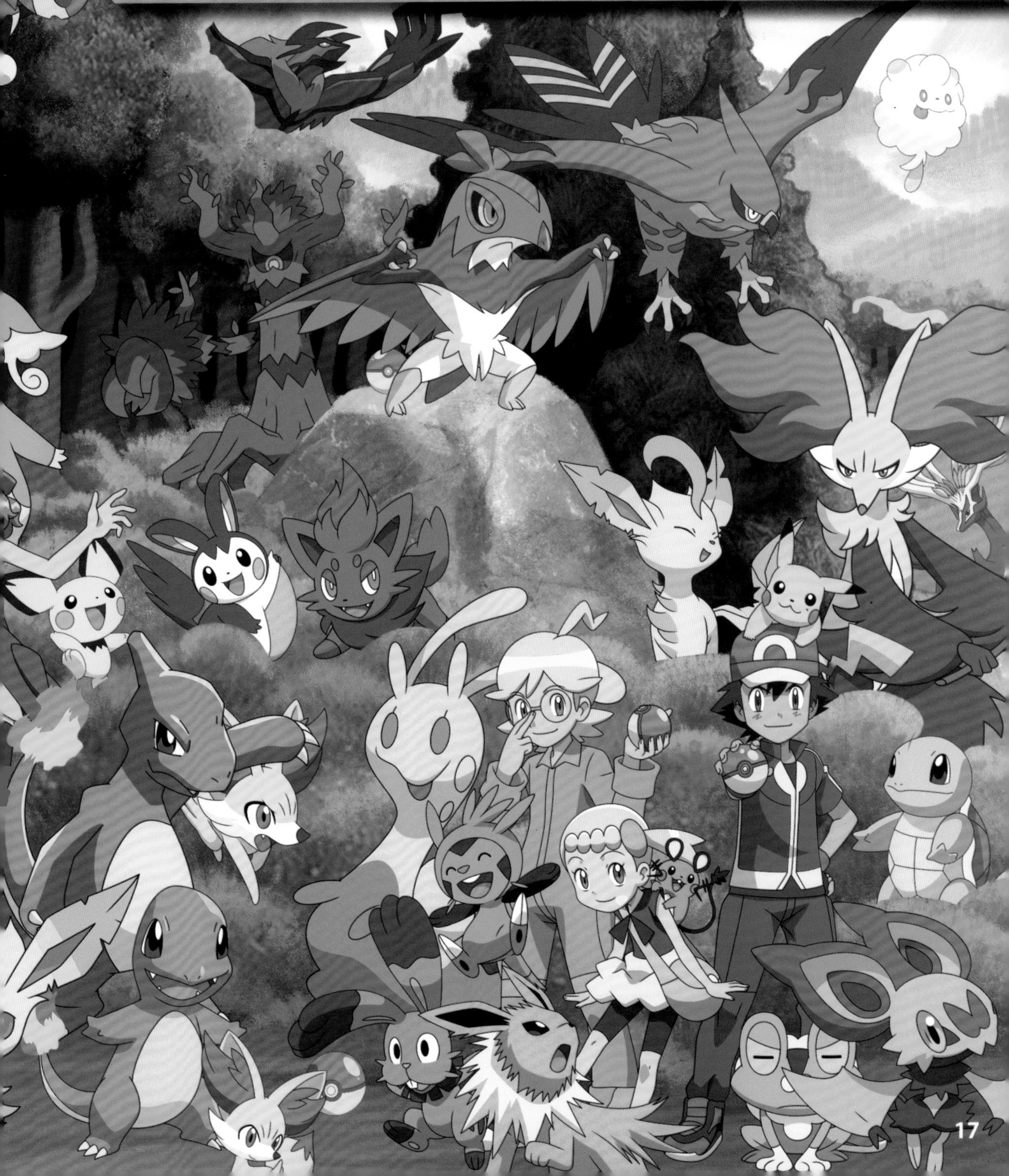

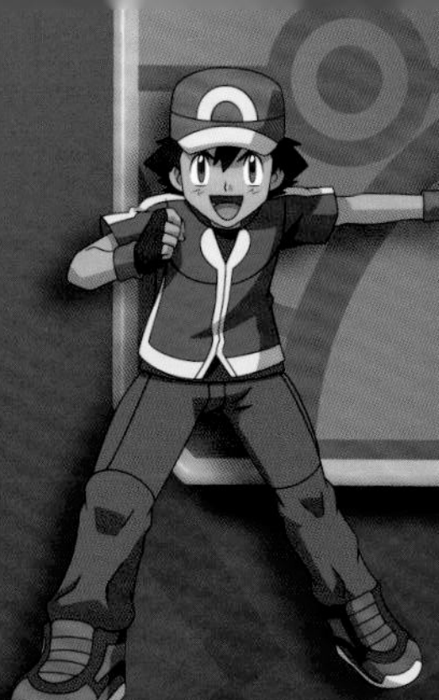

THE ULTIMATE CHALLENGE

Have you completed your mission and found all of the Pokémon in each of the scenes? If so, you're ready for the next challenge! Only the most exceptional Pokémon Trainers will succeed!

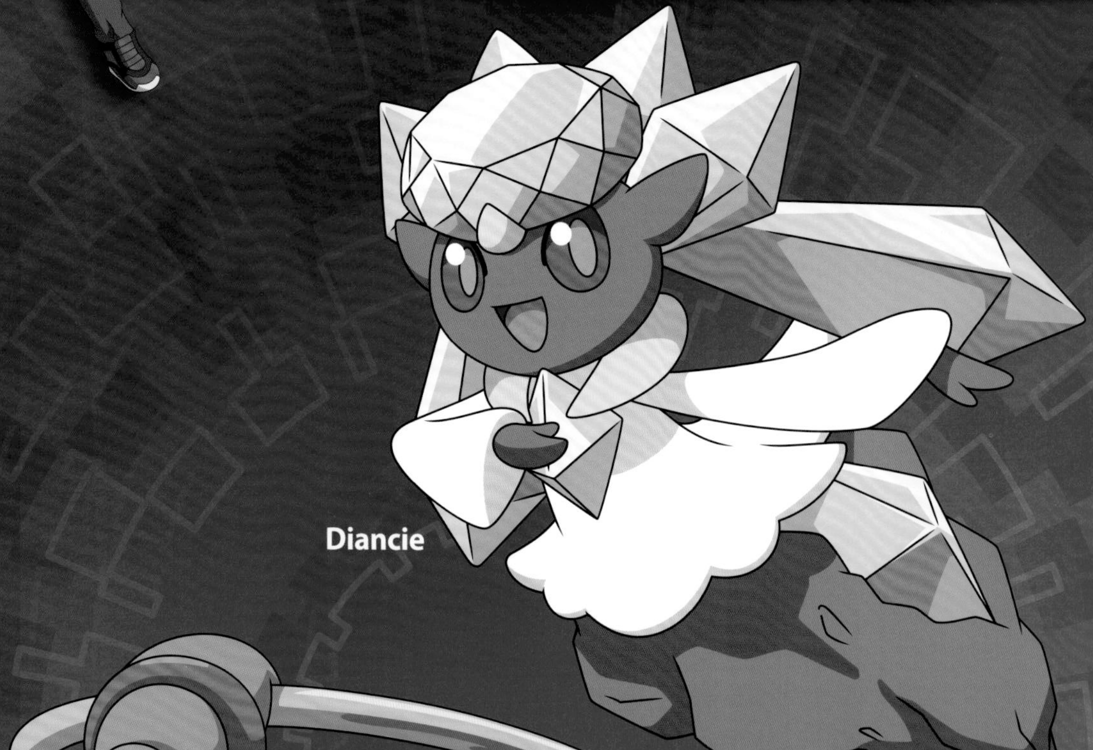
Diancie
Hoopa

Diancie and Hoopa appear throughout this story.

IT'S TIME TO FIND THEM!

CATEGORY:
NINJA POKÉMON

TYPE: WATER-DARK

HEIGHT: 4'11"

WEIGHT: 88.2 lbs

GRENINJA

Greninja can transform powerful sprays of water into an actual shuriken that it can propel at its enemies. With the cunning of a ninja, it hides in the shadows waiting to attack.

Froakie → Frogadier → **Greninja**

CHESNAUGHT

When its friends are in trouble, Chesnaught uses its own body like a shield. Its shell is strong enough to withstand the most powerful explosions.

Chespin → Quilladin → **Chesnaught**

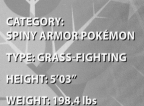

CATEGORY:
SPINY ARMOR POKÉMON

TYPE: GRASS-FIGHTING

HEIGHT: 5'03"

WEIGHT: 198.4 lbs

ZYGARDE CORE

Zygarde can take different Formes.

TALONFLAME

Talonflame can quickly melt itself onto its enemies when attacked. In extreme combat, its wings spread embers as it takes flight.

Fletchling → Fletchinder → **Talonflame**

CATEGORY:
SCORCHING POKÉMON

TYPE: FIRE-FLYING

HEIGHT: 3'11"

WEIGHT: 54.0 lbs

CATEGORY:
FOX POKÉMON

TYPE: FIRE-PSYCHIC

HEIGHT: 4'11"

WEIGHT: 86.0 lbs

DELPHOX

The mystical Delphox uses a fire-lit stick to achieve psychic visions. This Pokémon can see the future when it looks into the fire.

Fennekin → Braixen → **Delphox**

19

CATEGORY:
LIFE POKÉMON

TYPE: FAIRY

HEIGHT: 9' 10"

WEIGHT: 474.0 lbs

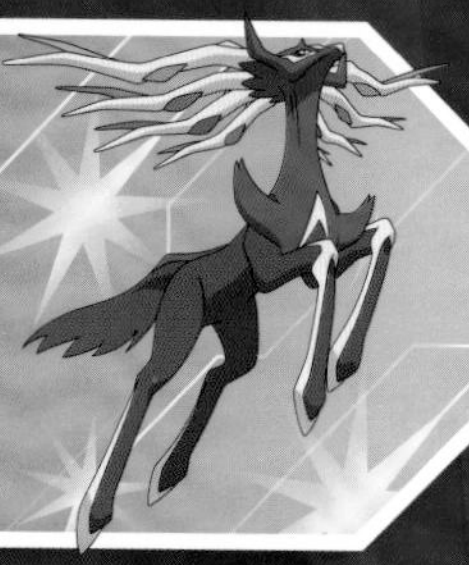

XERNEAS

Xerneas's horns light up in all the colors of the rainbow. It is said that this Legendary Pokémon can bestow eternal life.

YVELTAL

When Yveltal unfurls its black wings, its feathers emit a red glow. They say this Legendary Pokémon can absorb the life force of its adversaries.

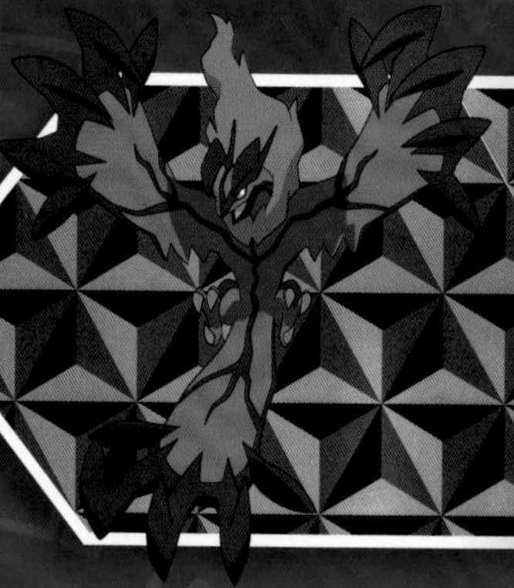

CATEGORY:
DESTRUCTION POKÉMON

TYPE: DARK-FLYING

HEIGHT: 19'00"

WEIGHT: 447.5 lbs

CATEGORY:
ORDER POKÉMON

TYPE: DRAGON-GROUND

HEIGHT: 16'05"

WEIGHT: 672.4 lbs

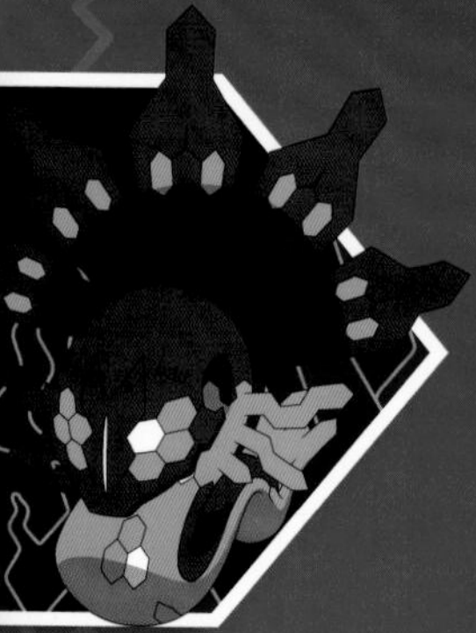

ZYGARDE 50% FORME

Zygarde lives in the caves of the Kalos region. They say this Legendary Pokémon is the guardian of the ecosystem.

Zygarde can take different Formes.

ZYGARDE 10% FORME

Zygarde can take different Formes.

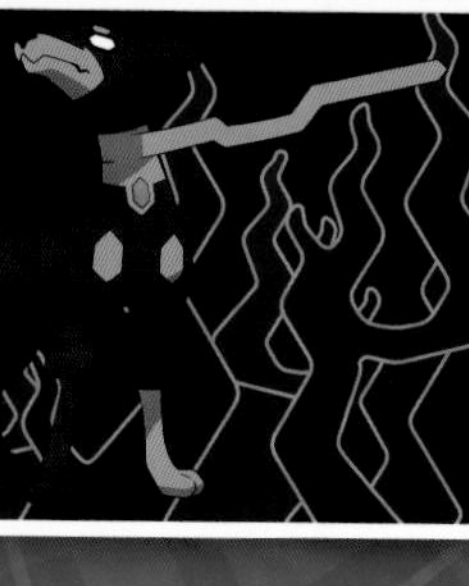

TYPE: DRAGON-GROUN

HEIGHT: 3'11"

WEIGHT: 73.9 lbs

TYPE: DRAGON-GROUND

HEIGHT: 14'09"

WEIGHT: 1344.8 lbs

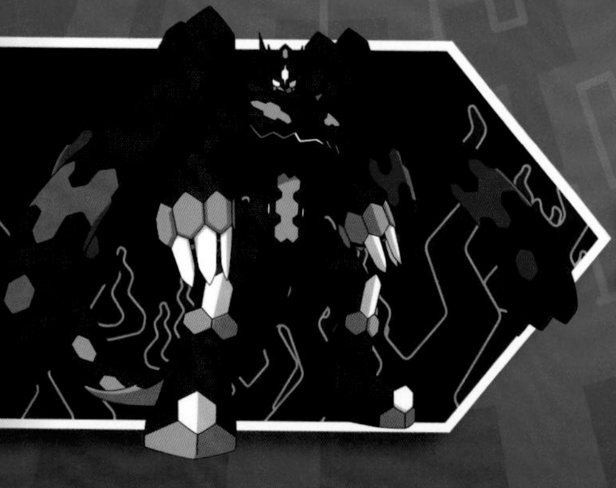

ZYGARDE COMPLETE FORME

Zygarde can take different Formes.

⊙ POKÉMON QUIZ

How well do you know your Pokémon? Are you ready to become a super Trainer? Answer these questions to find out!

① Seek and find at least four Psychic-type Pokémon in the scene on pages 10–11.

....

....

② Name the three Legendary Pokémon of Kalos.

....

....

③ What is the Evolution of Surskit?

Hint: Find it on pages 4 and 5.

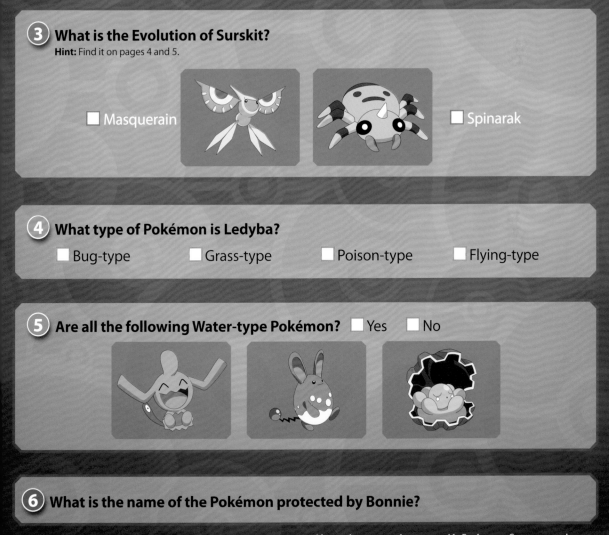

☐ Masquerain   ☐ Spinarak

④ What type of Pokémon is Ledyba?

☐ Bug-type   ☐ Grass-type   ☐ Poison-type   ☐ Flying-type

⑤ Are all the following Water-type Pokémon?   ☐ Yes   ☐ No

⑥ What is the name of the Pokémon protected by Bonnie?

Answers: 1. Meditite, Gardevoir, Gallade, and Meowstic (although all but Meowstic are dual-types). **2.** Xerneas, Yveltal, and Zygarde. **3.** Masquerain. **4.** Bug- and Flying-type. **5.** No, Wynaut is a Psychic-type Pokemon. **6.** Dedenne.

21

EXPLORE THE WORLD OF POKÉMON

There are many paths through the Kalos region. But wait... These scenes have been mixed up! One of these strips does not appear in this book. Can you find it?

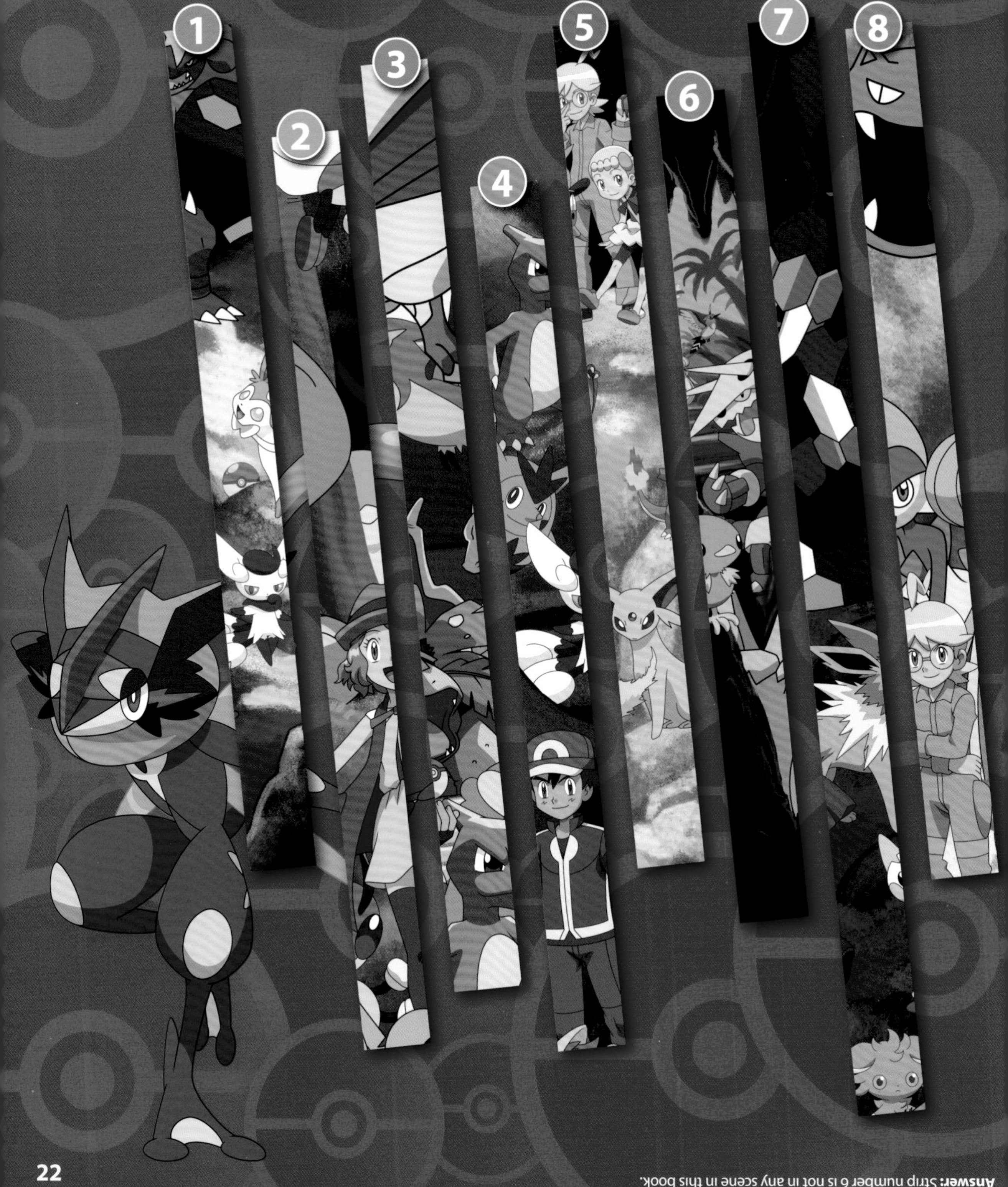
1
2
3
4
5
6
7
8

Answer: Strip number 6 is not in any scene in this book.

LEGENDARY MAZE

Ash wants to join Zygarde. Help him find his way!

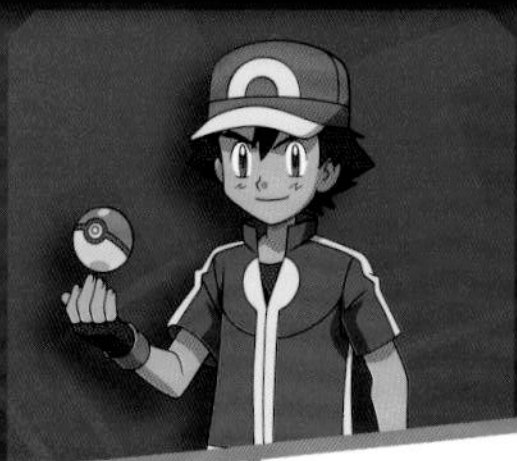

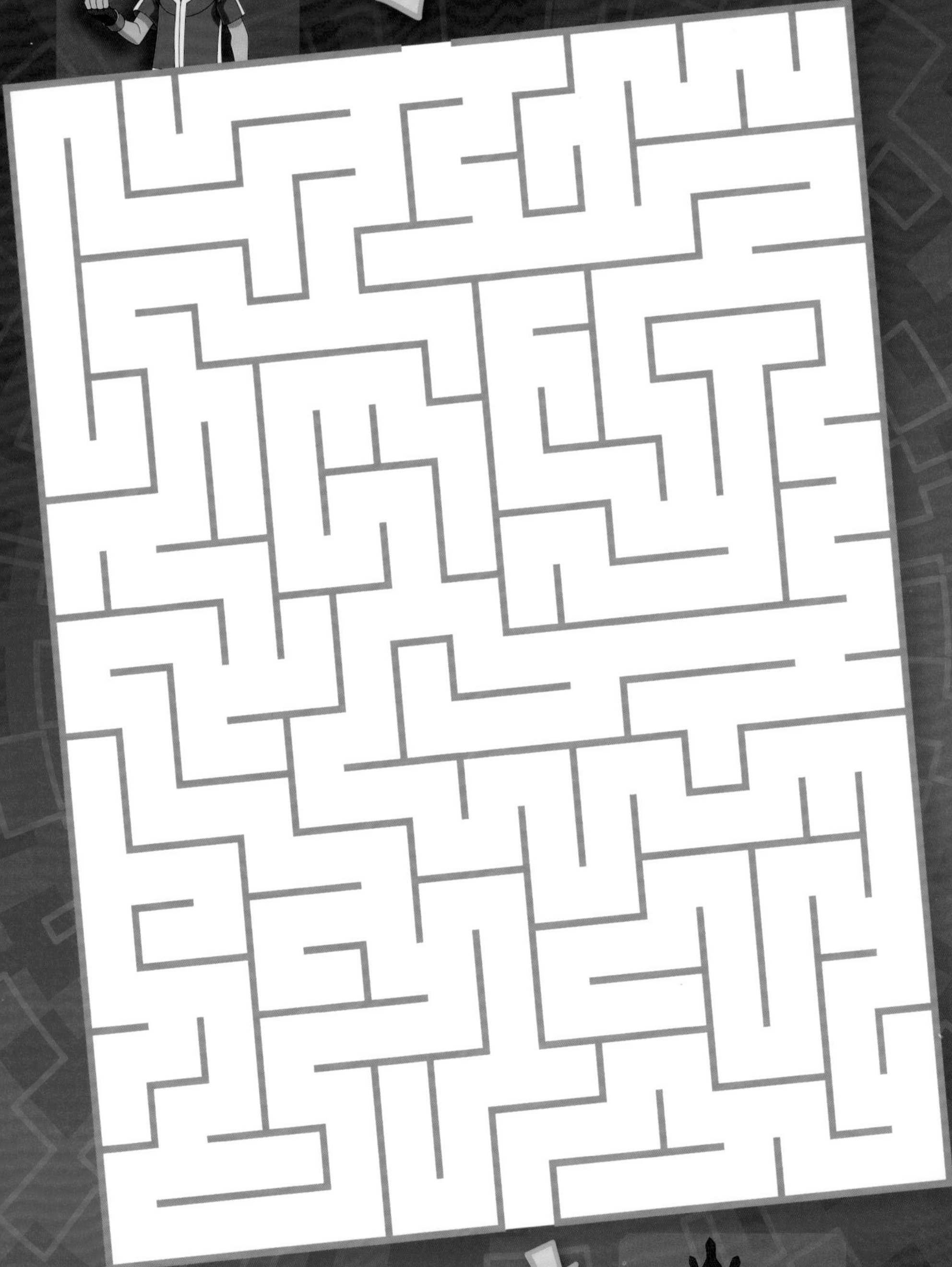

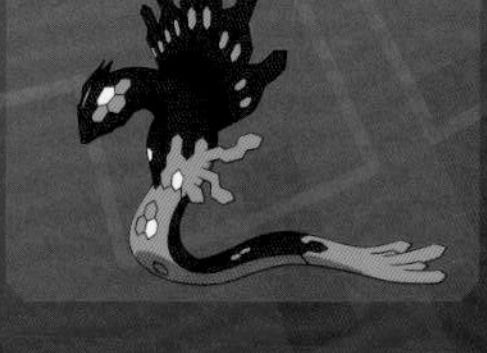

Solution on page 29.

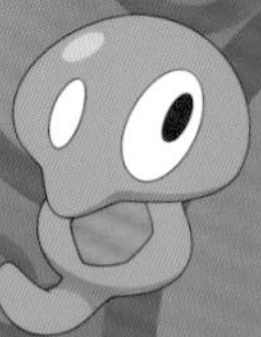

ALONE IN THE WORLD

One of these Pokémon doesn't have a match. Which one is it?

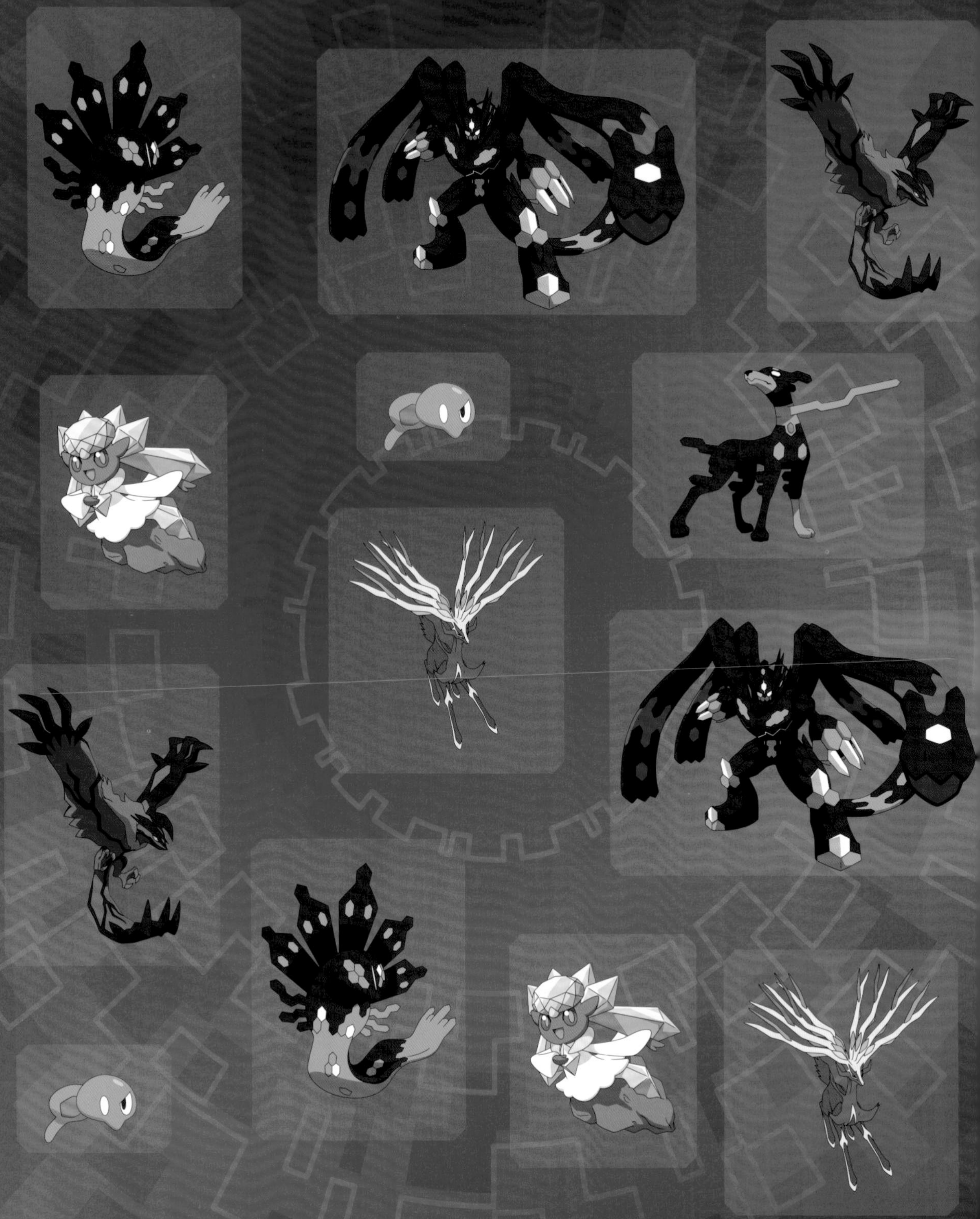

nswer: The Pokémon without a double is Zygarde 10% Forme.

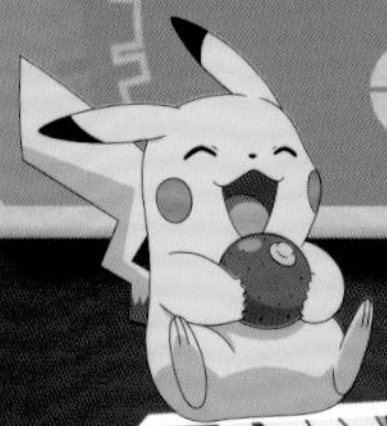

THE LEGENDARY POKÉMON OF KALOS

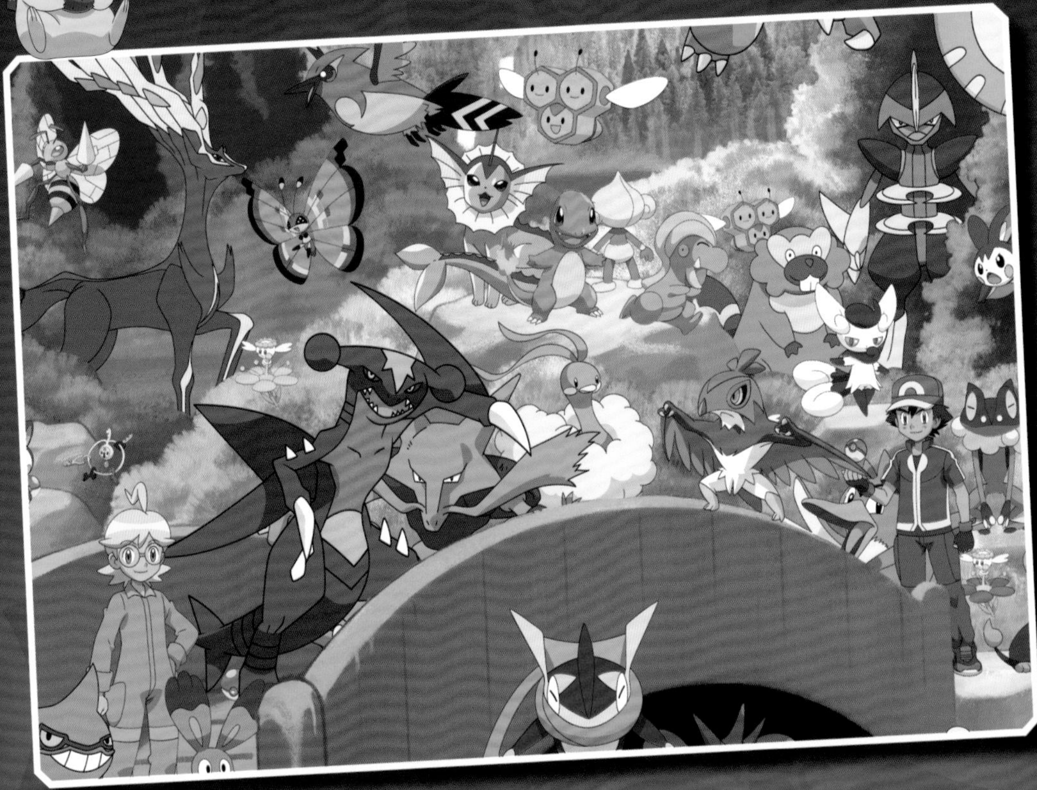

QUESTION 1: Xerneas is what type of Pokémon?

- ■ Psychic-type
- ■ Fairy-type
- ■ Normal-type

QUESTION 2: Yveltal is more than twenty feet tall. True or false?

QUESTION 3: How many Formes are there of Zygarde?

- ■ 3
- ■ 4
- ■ 5
- ■ 6

QUESTION 4: According to legend, what can Xerneas offer?

QUESTION 5: When Yveltal unfurls its wings, what color do its feathers glow?

- ■ Black
- ■ Red
- ■ White

Look very carefully at the image for a couple of minutes and then turn the page…

Answers: 1. Fairy-type. **2.** False. **3.** 5 (including Zygarde Cell). **4.** It can offer eternal life. **5.** Red.

OBSERVATION SKILLS

Did you get a good look at the scene on the previous page? Are you sure? Let's find out! Check true or false for each statement without turning the page back.

	TRUE	FALSE
Xerneas is in the scene.	■	■
Ash is holding a Poké Ball.	■	■
Serena is next to Clemont.	■	■
More than ten Pokémon are in the scene.	■	■
Vaporeon is next to Charmeleon.	■	■
Hawlucha is in the scene.	■	■
Clemont is with his sister.	■	■

CORRECT EVOLUTION

Complete this chain of Evolution for Gastly with the Pokémon below.

Gastly → ? ________ → ? ________ → ? ________

Mega Gengar

Haunter

Gengar

swers: True, True, False, True, False, True, False.
stly → Haunter → Gengar → Mega Gengar.

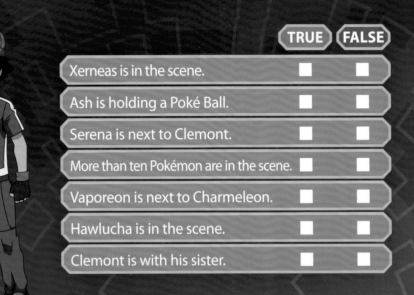

SUDOKUS

Complete the following sudoku puzzles using the stickers in this book. But be careful not to repeat Pokémon in either columns or rows!

SUDOKU 1

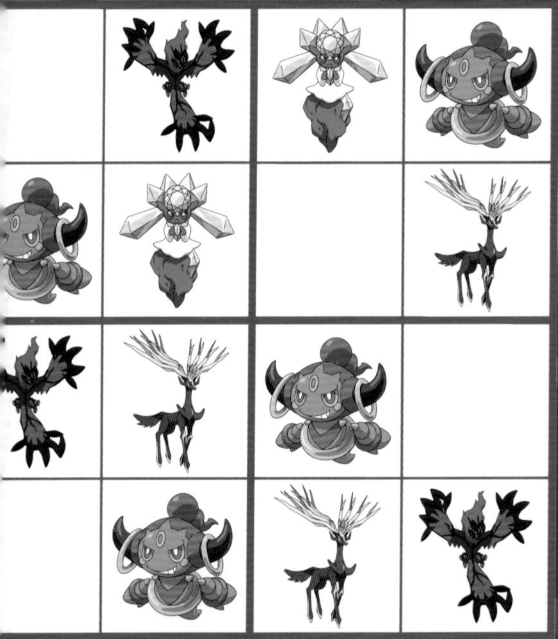

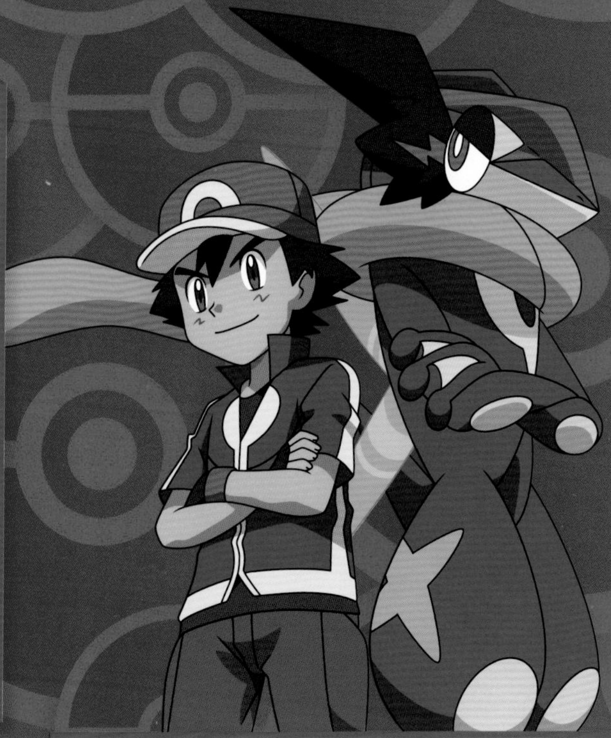

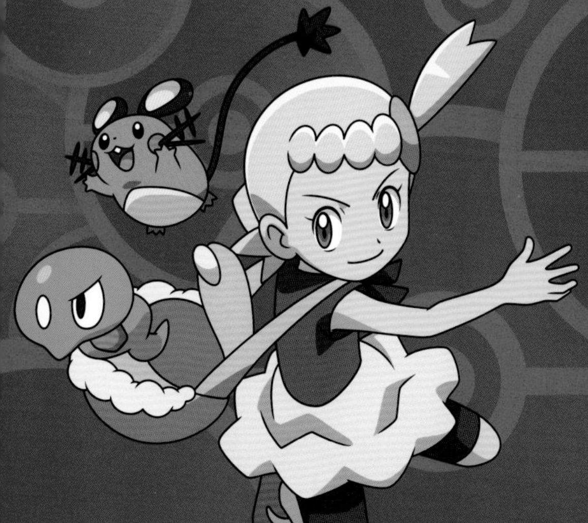

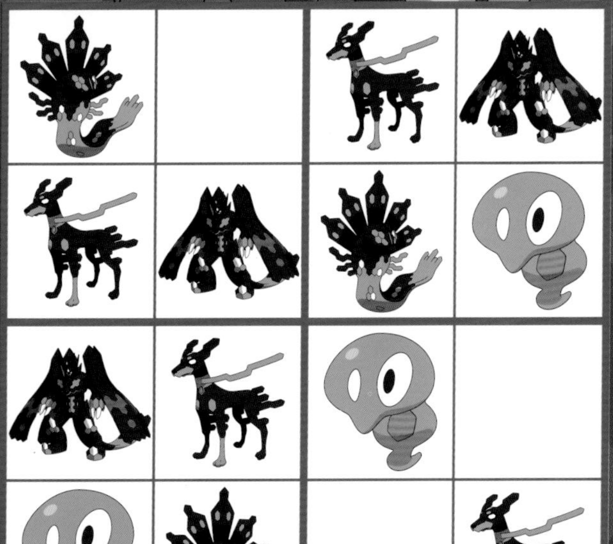

SUDOKU 2

Solutions on page 29.

SPOT THE DIFFERENCES

Find the seven differences between these two images.

Solution on page 29.